HIP SET

MICHAEL FERTIK

STIRLING PUBLISHING

978-1-912818-08-2 Hardback Edition

978-1-912818-10-5 Ebook

A catalogue record for this book is available from the British Library.

All characters and events in this book are fictitious. Any similarity to real persons, living or dead, is coincidental and not intended by the author.

Cover design by Mudlark Studio

Copy editing and typesetting by Mary Chesshyre and Andrew Chapman, Prepare to Publish Ltd

Printed and bound in the United Kingdom by Clays (London)

First printing July 2019

Published by Stirling Publishing, 10 Davidson House, 57 Queen Charlotte Street, Edinburgh EH6 7EY

www.stirlingpublishing.co.uk

For Zoe
Of the Same Day

ACKNOWLEDGMENTS

Kobi from La Mer.
Tabatha and her Stirling crew.
The Library Bar at the Norman TLV.
Of course, my family.

ONE

Oscar Orleans had concluded, after twenty years of living in Israel, that he had come here for the hips. Israeli women had the best hips in the world. It wasn't the asses or the busts or (certainly) the arms. It was the section from the low back to the upper ass, and the casual, forward-pressing, urgent swing in their walk. He could admire them all day.

It was a game he played with himself. None other than G–d Almighty had ordained his destiny to arrive in Israel so that he might discover and sing the praises of the Israeli female hip set. He blinked and laughed to himself. That line would never get old. No other explanation for his life made more sense.

Ding! Oscar looked up sharply at the woman at the next table sitting in a bright yellow bikini top and a brighter yellow sarong. She was smoking a fresh cigarette and wearing expansive sunglasses. She picked up her phone to look at the SMS or WhatsApp. She was what you'd call healthy, a small roll folding on her waistline as she sat, but he hated that sound so much he decided immediately that she was fat. That bell, that single ding that announced the arrival of a new phone message, was the most baneful noise pollution Oscar could name. He wished it could be uninvented.

It made him look at his own phone. There were three messages waiting for him. That was unusual. 7:33, Shabbat morning; who would want to reach him? Normally he could rely on this time: get any seat you want at La Mer beach bar, put your toes in the sand, drink Americano, notice the occasional umbrella going up and hip walking by, and no one would stare and wonder at your blackness. He looked at his phone again and out at Bugrashov Beach and felt his day was about to change.

Bob Marley piped quietly over the speakers. He glanced at the wait staff mustering cigarettes at the start or end of their shifts. It was since his arrival twenty years earlier – even in the last ten – that the trend of massive shin tattoos had appeared amid the hashish Rastafarian twenty-something idiot hip set. Dreadlocked kids high on hash or pills 24/7 earning enough to pay for plane tickets to India and Jamaica where they could grow tattoo collections and sip and preach universal love for a few more years. Freedom, he thought to himself. When he had first arrived, he'd thought the beach bar working youth were mentally ill. Then he had admired them their devil-may-care. Then he had developed a soft spot. It was natural, wasn't it, or understandable. You're just out of the army. You've spent the last two years holding a rifle. Half the world hates you for being what you are. You've never left the country before, and one hundred million people living on your borders would celebrate your demise. Housing is unaffordable in Tel Aviv. You haven't started your education. Why wouldn't your mind wander to Pacific Islander tattoo motifs and an imagined Caribbean fantasy of a failed drug culture? What more constructive response could you choose than to love everyone on the planet equally, even if they would never really love you back? You had to admire these Israelis. Even the lazy hashish beach staff.

He closed his eyes for one second to reset and embrace the soft sea air.

"Shit," he said aloud. All the messages were from Kobi Sambinsky.

Mefake'ah Kobi Sambinsky. Inspector Sambinsky.

"Call me" said the first one, time stamped at 6:49 a.m.

"Urgent" was the next one in the same minute.

"Oscar wake up" had come in ten minutes later.

He dialed.

"Hello," Sambinsky answered, after less than one ring. "I'm at the Dolphinarium. Can you come now?"

"Shabbat shalom."

"Yes, Shabbat shalom, Oscar. It's serious. You'd better come."

"Fifteen minutes."

Oscar picked up his canvas satchel. He wished he wasn't wearing flip flops. He rose and headed south on Herbert Samuel.

His destination was a kilometer down the *tayelet*, the boardwalk, just the stretch from Bugrashov Beach to Banana Beach to Blue Bird Beach, basically. But it was decades away in spacetime.

The Dolphinarium was the biggest structure on the beach in all of Tel Aviv. Since 2001, when Saeed Hotari, a twenty-two-year-old affiliated with Hamas, had blown himself up killing twenty-one people – the majority of them teenage girls whose families had immigrated from Russia – this former discotheque, famous and cavernous, had become a national blight, staying mostly empty, destroyed, decaying and deteriorating, slowly encroached upon and then covered by graffiti artists who started by commemorating the massacre and later just did regular shitty tagging. Now it was nothing. A car rental place had taken over one corner of the usable lot, and a tiny section had been reborn as a desultory night club from time to time. But this huge shipwreck of a building in the best location of the country remained, as did so much in Tel Aviv, inexplicably unsold and undeveloped.

For Oscar, and for so many sabras and immigrants alike, this one place betrayed a thousand streams of the Israeli story. Russian immigrant kids getting blown up by a terrorist whose explosives launched ball bearings and iron washers that ripped through their bodies. It was the incident that convinced Prime Minister Ariel Sharon to commence plans for a barrier wall along Israel's border to prevent the infiltration of future suicide bombers. Meanwhile steel and glass hotels and residential towers had sprung up in the years since. Madonna and Kim Kardashian had bought apartments within a few hundred meters. The country's best fish restaurant, a Scandinavian-looking spot serving contemporary Israeli food, was next door. Israel had moved on from the massacre, and hadn't. Tel Aviv had become a cosmopolitan city for the glitterati at the same moment it had sealed its doors. This country of hounded, vagabonded, abandoned, maltreated, wandering souls, whose people had never not been refugees, started, perhaps imperceptibly at first, to allow itself to worry about what it meant to have permissive borders.

At the very moment when the global growth of high tech catapulted Israel from a developing economy into a wealthy state, making it a hugely attractive dream destination for destitute workers seeking better lives, it took a turn inwards. And now, some sorry African fucker, far from home and no doubt scared witless, had done something terribly wrong at the Dolphinarium, or worse, had been killed in that desolate spot for a cause still unknown.

That was the only reason they would have summoned Oscar early on a Saturday morning.

TWO

The corpse looked peaceful except for the bullet wound in the stomach and the other one in the head. He was late teens, maybe twenty, rail skinny and probably more than 190 centimeters if he were laid flat, which he wasn't.

What a place to die. This sweaty, moldy, blank corner of grey cinder block, smelling of generations of piss and alcoholic vomitus. Light bouncing off the Mediterranean glinted through the crumbling concrete and rebar bent by time and hooligans. Oscar breathed through his mouth and tried to catch the notes of sea salt air on his tongue. He had learned how to respire in foul-smelling conditions as a child. It was one of his oldest memories. This poor creature, from some village outside Juba or Rumbek, he guessed, had made it the four and a half thousand kilometers to Tel Aviv, on a journey that probably required him to cover twice that, to find the end of his life in an open toilet. Trade one hell for another. *Always Africans get the short end. The whole world seems designed to fuck us.*

"No," Oscar answered. Sambinsky wanted to know if he recognized the victim.

"Anything?"

"Probably a recent arrival. You don't have his ID?"

"No ID. We'll get the face to the border patrol, see if they have him in the computer. Why recent?"

"His shirt." Oscar knelt down to get a closer look. "It's the South Sudan away shirt for next season. I don't think he ordered it online."

"What are you looking for?" Sambinsky crouched next to him. His belly squeezed against his belt. He always felt conscious of his belly when he was around Africans. And he was around Africans on most days. Though he usually didn't have to crouch.

"See his pants? The tear in the pocket has been mended many times. This is probably his only set of clothes."

Sambinsky looked up at the young woman in uniform who was hovering behind him. She caught his glance and made to jot down notes in a black flipbook.

"May I?" Oscar held a pen out right next to the young man's collar as if to lift it.

"Yeah, we've got all the photographs we wanted while we were waiting for you to show up."

Oscar looked at Sambinsky's twinkling eye but decided not to call him a schmuck, which was what he probably wanted. He had come to love the Israelis in nearly all their flavors, and in many moments he would smile at the rough tenderness of the Eastern European Jewish culture. But he had found it didn't suit him to participate. Politeness was too much of his DNA. And while he had come to understand the Jewish instinct for humor in even the most macabre settings as a powerful coping mechanism in a four-thousand-year history of too many macabre settings one after the other, he had long ago concluded that his own formality – and his solemnity around the dead – made more sense to him. On many occasions, his formality had saved his life and his sanity. He could hardly abandon it.

He could tell from Sambinsky's crestfallen face that the policeman was now worried he'd caused some form of offense. Oscar decided not to let him off the hook.

Sambinsky would get over it fast and could just as easily come back with more if he felt excused.

"He's Toposa," Oscar said, his pen lifting the shirt enough to see the man's shoulder. Sambinsky shone a light from his cellphone. Oscar heard the sharp intake of breath. Vertical rows of elevated scars the size of one-shekel coins and looking like blisters reached the top of the scapula. Oscar moved the pen to the waistline and lifted the bottom of the soccer jersey. The lady police gave a short cry. More than twenty rows of healed wounds ran down his chest and belly. There were hundreds of them.

"Tribal scarification. This style is Toposa. He probably got it when he was twelve or thirteen."

He felt the tension ease. He knew Sambinsky, at least, had seen tribal scarring before around Tel Aviv, though nothing this extensive.

"Toposa?" Sambinsky stood and stretched his hamstrings.

"It is a tribe in southeast Sudan. Herders. I've never seen one here before. He might be the only one."

"What is he doing here?" the girl asked out loud.

Oscar faced her. "These guys don't typically come here. They have no education, no schooling. Toposa are pastoral. They mostly stay to themselves. No, that's not quite right. I mean there is no way for them to do any differently. They raise their cattle, graze their cattle, and they get into fights with their neighbors when they steal their cattle."

"They fight which neighbors?" The young woman looked eager to jot down a motive in her flipbook.

"Toposa aren't frequently fleeing as refugees?" Sambinsky

sounded curious. Equally as to the answer and as to why anyone in South Sudan would not want to flee. Oscar nodded. Sambinsky was *navon* – wise; they understood each other.

"It's interesting. Toposa were one of the few tribes that fought for both sides over the years. They are determinedly unconvertible. Nearly all of them continue to reject Islam and Christianity. So they had no natural enemies in the conflict."

"Nor friends," Sambinsky said.

"Nor friends. In fact, one might say they went out of their way to make enemies of everyone. From that perspective, they could easily want to flee before or after the partition."

The young woman lowered her flipbook, sensing that she wasn't going to record a motive and that they were about to get into a car to drive to South Tel Aviv.

"But that is what is curious," Oscar said aloud.

"What?" Sambinsky looked at him.

"Even if the Toposa are under threat, they don't leave. It's not clear where a Toposa would get a football shirt, let alone the means to travel across Africa, set aside the cash to pay Bedouin to smuggle him across the border." Oscar paused. "I know someone we can talk to about this."

"We're going to see Kuur?" Sambinsky asked.

"The man of G–d himself," Oscar replied.

THREE

"He was only around for one week or two weeks. I did not meet him. But I did have occasion to lay eyes upon him more than once."

Oscar liked Michael Kuur, who was more properly known as Michael Alou Kuur Kuur and who had started calling himself Pastor Michael at some point in the past decade and a half since his arrival in Tel Aviv. To be sure it had elevated Kuur among his countrymen. And Oscar speculated that Kuur in turn speculated that it would elevate his position with the Israelis. That much was probably true of the orthodox Jews, with whom Kuur would almost certainly have irregular contact, and untrue of the social services and police, with whom Kuur would almost certainly have extremely regular contact. Pastor Michael gave the impression of always knowing more than he said and of enjoying the process of revealing the innards of the onion one layer at a time. This made it fun to talk with him. Oscar liked, too, that Michael had not adapted his speech patterns to the locals' predilection for speed and shorthand. The pastor never used contractions, and he spoke both languorously and elegantly, a product of the British university system that had educated the aristocratic members of the Dinka tribe for some generations. Listening to him was therefore also fun. Then visiting Pastor Michael Kuur was fun, too, as he was always to be found in his own makeshift and illegal storefront on Neve Sha'anan Street, which he excused as a "private club" called Jebena where he served and purportedly sold cups of guhwah, the Sudanese coffee with cloves, to anyone who might like to sit and enjoy the air conditioning. Kuur had fitted out the room with chairs, low tables, cushions, and rugs. He had placed among these accouterments one slightly higher seat, which he reserved for himself. It looked enough like a throne to reinforce his role as the semi-official elder of the city's Sudanese community. Finally, Oscar liked knowing the pastor because, while he might be in charge of a tidy side business in whatever it was, and while he might not be described as, say, unarmed, he had never been reputed to abuse his people, who were largely helpless to predation. Oscar would not have called him a man of G–d, but nor was he the other thing. On the contrary, the rumors tended to say Kuur kept the peace and put a quick stop to violence, lest the locals grow agitated and insist on the immediate deportation of the remaining Sudanese.

Sambinsky liked him for much the same reasons. More than once he had kept Kuur out of jail by explaining to his superiors just how helpful the pastor was in keeping the crime rate low. Sambinsky's entire Asylum Unit was four people. Without Kuur, he would probably need a dozen. Usually that arithmetic alone was enough to get his commanders to leave the man be.

"Tell us what you know." Sambinsky poured coffee and handed the cup to his adjutant before helping himself.

"He called himself Deng, though it is very unlikely in the utmost that this was his real name," Kuur said.

"Why?"

"Deng is a Dinka name. A distinctly Dinka name, in fact," Oscar replied.

"Just so," Michael nodded. "But I also heard that he had allowed himself to be called Kinga."

"That is very curious." Oscar raised his fingers to his chin in contemplation. Sambinsky smiled. He had on several occasions sought to explain to his wife how the African refugees, in physical and oral expression, often exuded the elegance of the characters from a 1940s American movie. She had grunted a response that she, for one, did not like American movies and that perhaps "the Americans would be happier than we to have the Africans over there with them." Eventually Sambinsky stopped telling her, but he still enjoyed it every time he saw it happen.

"What is it, Oscar?" he asked.

"There was a very famous Toposa named Kinga. Kinga Longokwo. It could imply this young man was a relation or that he wanted to be known as one."

"He was a chief?" Sambinsky asked.

"Father Kinga Longokwo," Kuur smiled. "He was the leader in the way of the Toposa. For a time. The Toposa do not have a precise concept corresponding to chief. But he was educated as a priest. This made him certainly a personage of great influence among his tribe. He died some years back. His position was not without controversy."

"What do you mean?" Sambinsky asked. His adjutant raised her flipbook again.

"He was a Catholic priest. For this reason perhaps alone the Western authorities who wished to deal with the Toposa were predisposed to deal with him. But of course they did not quite realize that he was inclined to inflate the number of Christian converts among his tribe." Kuur started to break out into another smile. Oscar joined him. "It might not be an exaggeration to say that Father Kinga's family was the only Catholic clan among the

Toposa. But without a doubt the Western officials who met with him would have come away with rather a different conclusion."

Now Oscar and Kuur began to chuckle out loud. Sambinsky had observed more than once that African refugees were ready to laugh gently at nearly any "white people can be such children" story. He couldn't blame them.

"You mean being Christian in Sudan in this period would not have been without controversy?"

"That much, yes," said Kuur. "But Kinga had his fair share of legitimacy. Before he persuaded his people to join the Christian separatist forces, he won their respect and admiration by convincing the political leaders in Khartoum to provide modern light weapons to his tribe. Once armed, he turned them upon the Sudanese central government by forming an alliance with the Sudan People's Liberation Army."

"Some priest," Sambinsky allowed.

"Yes." Kuur laughed a little louder and stood up to refresh his coffee. "A most unusual individual. It may also be possible that he had occasion to have some progeny of his own—"

"Perhaps in his retirement," Oscar interjected with a smile.

"Indeed, well stated, perhaps in his retirement from the priesthood."

Sambinsky let the facts settle for a second.

"That's all we've got? He sometimes let himself get called by the same name as Father Kinga?"

Oscar nodded in such a way as to convey he understood and affirmed the gravity of the subject. Then he continued. "It is not just a name." He turned to Sambinsky and looked him in the eyes. "Kinga was very famous. It would be perceived as presumptuous and not tributary to name a Toposa child after him during his lifetime if he was not a relation. It is possible that this young man simply wanted to be a relation or to be understood as one."

"Ah." Sambinsky sat and crossed his legs at the knee.

"But something starts to come together. Perhaps only a Toposa from this type of family would have the means to make his way here."

"Please show me those photographs once again." Pastor Kuur leaned forward to hold the phone. He traced the scarring on the man's torso and shoulders with his finger. Then he flipped through the photos left and right.

"There is no scarring on his arms," he said, looking up at the others. Sambinsky noticed Kuur also searched the eyes of his adjutant, as if looking for confirmation. "I should have noticed that before."

Sambinsky felt lost. "*Nu?*" So *what?*

"So what kind of Toposa would have perfect markings on his torso, abdomen, and shoulders yet none on his arms? Normally it extends all the way down to one's wrists." Oscar stepped forward next to Kuur's chair and looked intently at the photos to double check his memory and the pastor's report. He brought his nose close to the screen as the pastor zoomed in further. "Nothing," he murmured in agreement.

"I have no clue," Sambinsky said quizzically.

"So he could live a life outside the Toposa." His aide's voice cut the room. The men looked up at her.

"This is Officer Cone," Sambinsky said.

"So she has a name," Oscar smiled in greeting. "I am Oscar Orleans." He extended his hand.

"Very nice to meet you," Cone replied and gushed a sudden smile, her heavy Ukrainian accent evident in every syllable.

Sambinsky had plucked her from rookie school on the basis of her exceptional scores in logical reasoning and analysis, and her fluency in six European and Near Eastern languages. Her marksmanship and judgment were abysmal. So were her scores for bravery, which explained why he was still startled when she spoke up. In the army she had been awarded a medal for identifying a female suicide bomber at a West Bank crossing. A bomber who had made it through three prior checkpoints. She had deduced the terrorist's status by noting that a woman with perfectly manicured nails, exceptionally clear skin, a dancer's gait, an aristocratic lower back arch, a chin line that never deviated from a parallel to the ground, long hair without a strand out of place, and brand new high-heeled shoes with no scuffing on the soles, was also wearing a huge shawl that was unstylishly if carefully wrapped around her midsection and arms. In her debrief, Angelika had recalled the threat assessment had taken her less than two seconds, about the duration of a once-over, but that she had struggled for over a minute to summon the courage to alert her superior. The mixture of acumen and paralysis was so acute that she had no future in the army unit. But she was given a medal of distinction and earned the name Sherlock Cones. To top it off, the bomber had been captured alive and turned informant. Angelika had correctly diagnosed the incongruity: ladies trained as dancers were rare in the territories and invariably from liberal families. This bomber had been pressed into service when her brother, a university student, had been killed by falling rubble from an Israeli Hellfire missile. He had been the hope of the family as well as the main breadwinner. Without him, they had no means of support. Hamas had acted swiftly to turn her, promising a lifetime of security for her parents, and set her out on the mission. The Israelis were able to turn her back and get her family the funds it needed to make it stick. In the intelligence community, this operation was rated a success, and it had all started with the eighteen-year-old Angelika "Sherlock" Cone. In Israel, in certain circles, Cone would never in her life have to worry about her livelihood.

"Say that again," Sambinsky looked at her.

"It's like punk kids or hipsters who tattoo their bodies but stop at their necks and armpits." As she reached the word armpit she looked around nervously to see if she had said something that was somehow rude. She saw only that they were looking at her. "They leave their arms natural so they can integrate with society and not get judged at work and things."

"That is precisely correct," said Kuur. "With the added complexity that, among the Toposa, the scarring process occurs around twelve years of age, hardly around the time when youth are making prudent long-term decisions for their futures."

"So someone is making the decision for them," said Sambinsky.

"His parents," Cone said.

"His rather aristocratic parents, we can surmise," said Kuur. "Parents who foresaw a future for their son away from southeast Sudan."

"Perhaps a future of literacy and of high school and even of university in the city. A future of wearing football shirts and of attaining enlightenment through education, and then perhaps priesthood and leadership."

"You mean this could be Father Kinga's kid."

"Or some such," Oscar nodded.

FOUR

For Oscar Orleans, it was perhaps not saying too much to observe that the scent of a first-world morgue was his most sincere reminder of his blessed good fortune.

First-world morgues smell different from third-world morgues. Oscar had learned this in his second year of residence in Israel, when he had visited the Ichilov Medical Center mortuary to act as an interpreter for the family of a deceased. Vividly he had recalled his only prior trip to a morgue, the National Forensic Processing Bureau in Kinshasa, to identify the body of his best friend Arthur. That journey had been made at the invitation of the government. Colonel Roland DuBest, whose charge was to suppress the university protests, personally picked up Oscar from his student housing, ferried him in an olive green Citroën CX to the morgue, and slowly revealed the extent of Arthur's head wounds. He had continued to undrape the corpse even after Oscar's positive identification, politely insisting that he take in the hemorrhaging evident all over his friend's body. The sadism had worked. By the morning, Oscar had fled Kinshasa, resigning his chairmanship of the University Freedom

Alliance by handwritten letter, never to return to the campus or city.

Even then and all this time since, Oscar experienced the memory of the wretched overpowering scent of that place with more revulsion than he did the well-lit, inescapable implosions that were once his friend's face. In the dozens of visits he had made over the years to Tel Aviv's various morgues, he had never failed to breathe in through his nostrils the clean, disinfected, antiseptic, overtly neutral or faintly acidic refrigerated air immediately upon entering. Each time he felt himself win a small incremental reprieve against the terror he carried with him of that time, of that final protest march and police mayhem, of his friend's disappearance and murder, of the life he nearly had, of the death he nearly shared. In time, Oscar had learned the ancient Jewish *bracha*, thanking G–d for the proper functioning of one's orifices. He had murmured it to himself at the Israeli morgues ever since. It was not something he could ever explain to anyone. It was even more difficult in his mind than explaining to an educated liberal Israeli why he had never known an educated liberal African who objected to the phrase "third world."

Sambinsky watched Oscar breathe deeply through his nose and realized that he had come to expect Oscar to make this little ritual. Then he felt a flash of bareness clutch his upper ribs, as he understood that he had visited the morgue enough times with Oscar Orleans to have learned to anticipate this idiosyncratic customary behavior upon their arrival. He had dubbed this feeling the Police Gloom, a sensation that detectives occasionally acknowledged to one another after a decade or more on the force. This was the nature of a friendship: to see a man you like most often in a place of death. This was the nature of a life: trips to mortuaries stacked one on top of the other until retirement. It was the sort of feeling that pervaded the Scandinavian police procedurals Sambinsky read during the rainy Januarys in Tel Aviv, with their divorced alcoholic investigators who all, ridiculously, liked opera and knew how to spell Dvorak. Sambinsky smiled and winced as he watched Oscar exhale, and understood he liked this lean, honest man from far away and that he was his friend and that this fluorescent, air conditioned basement of formaldehyde was the nature of their friendship.

"Inspector Sambinsky, you are absolutely welcome to step into the main room next to me for purpose of viewing victim and receive draft preliminary report. You also are invited, Officer Cone and Mr. Orleans." The diminutive Dr. Niyazova smiled guilelessly and waved a beckoning left arm, which just perceptibly creased her starched white coat. Niyazova had immigrated from Uzbekistan as a teenager and still spoke broken Hebrew. She called herself Shimrit, which Sambinsky knew was not her real name, but how could he blame her, a Jew returning to her homeland for the first time since probably the Babylonian exile. She'd come here, found an education as a forensic pathologist, and made her way to the chief medical examiner's office. Sambinsky figured that, in her logic, it was a good career for someone who wanted to be a wife and mother, and it probably was in some corner of reasoning or another. Old cultures and new jobs mixed like that in immigrant countries. He allowed himself to be proud of her and Israel when he saw her. Besides, she was good to look at. Broad face, cheekbones up near the moon, eyes the size of espresso saucers, and a skin complexion like milk chai, smooth even under the hundred and twenty cycles pulsing through the pasty overhead bulbs. She was late twenties, unmarried. Sambinsky sighed and sucked in his gut.

"What do we have?" he asked in a gruff voice, seeking to reestablish his authority, most of all for himself, and sensing immediately that he had overpowered it.

"He was probably eighteen to twenty years, but could be younger. Healthy. But nutrition not developed country. He had some alcohol in blood. No drugs. He has many scars you have seen already. They are symmetrical and healed a long time." Oscar peered down at the young man's cleaned-up face. He imagined what he had looked like as a child growing up in the grassland of South Sudan, what his smile had looked like when he greeted his mother as a young boy after a day of play or the chore of watering cattle. He closed his eyes and forced away the image. It was too horrible.

"I have made discovery of probable interesting to you, Inspector." Niyazova straightened up just a little, as if preparing to present her findings at a conference. She lifted a tray from her pathologist's table and moved it under their noses. "Procedural inspection indicated the recent amateur surgery on this tooth. I removed it with care after discovery it was not fixed in place."

Sambinsky saw the molar and noticed immediately that its root had been hollowed out. He glanced at Oscar.

"Where is it?" Oscar asked.

Niyazova smiled and stepped to a locked cabinet and withdrew a tiny plastic box. She tweezed the contents and held something up to the light. Then she dropped it carefully into the tooth's cavity, where it rested and reflected the overhead bulb.

"Gold!" Sambinsky exclaimed. "He had gold in his tooth."

"I have seen it before," Oscar nodded. "Previously only with diamonds. Smugglers will use the tooth to conceal a sample of the merchandise on a scouting trip to be deployed for emergency use when some bribe or payment is needed."

Sambinsky had seen it before, too, but only in a police briefing, never the real thing. Niyazova thrust the tray into his hands and eased open the victim's mouth. She pointed a small lamp and depressed the tongue with a pen. The molar second from the back on the top right-hand side was missing. To

Sambinsky's eyes, the opening looked raw and painful but not infected, but what did he know.

"So our boy was a smuggler?" Sambinsky asked.

"Our boy was a smuggler," Niyazova nodded and smiled, rejoicing in her contribution more than in the conclusion. She beamed at the detective, who felt self-conscious about his reaction to her and directed his eyes to Oscar.

Oscar didn't look so sure.

FIVE

Oscar stepped outside the shul and sniffed the sycamore tree above his head. It was mixed with the city scents of a Tel Aviv September: diesel, heat, sand, moisture from human and atmospheric sweat, sea salt, the notional beginning of rotting leaves, somewhere a cigarette, somewhere a trash bag, stray cats, and evening-blooming flowers.

The men brushed past him down the three steps to Yavne Street, at the bottom of Nahmani. It was 6:30 p.m., and the idea of dusk was arriving in the light that reflected off the white Bauhaus buildings across the quiet two-lane road. Three blocks away was Rothschild Boulevard and the bustling celebratory launch of another bustling celebratory Saturday evening in the most fervent nightlife in the Middle East. But here it was a small town with a single car passing and then only the noises of men leaving prayer. Tel Aviv was like that. Move a few hundred meters, and you could find a different tempo and maybe a different century.

The other men emerging from the shul were dressed like 18th-century Polish nobles. Hundreds of years ago, their Haredi ancestors had adopted the black coats and fur hats of the local nobility, and the habit had continued ever since. In the Israeli heat, in the confines of a synagogue, it made for a sweaty setting, despite the air conditioning. Oscar paused on the second step as usual. The Hasidim largely ignored him and one another as they strolled home. Some clasped their hands behind their backs, tilted forward, and murmured prayers or stared down at their feet in contemplation, looking overall very much like the portraits of themselves you might find in the artist stalls at the Mahne Yehuda near the knockoff Chagalls. One, a fifty-something Jew named Hirschy Zarchi, shouted, *"Oy vavoy oy oy oy vavoy!"* over and over as he walked down the street, erupting with a lamentation or jubilation carried over from his evening prayers, no one could tell, except him and his G–d.

Oscar had tried many synagogues when he had first sought conversion, and many more since. The Yemeni one on Khanokh Street, the Conservative one on Morits Daniel, a Reform one on Rashi, the American one on Ben Yehuda, the French one on Bar Kokhva, and a couple of others for the Hasidim. For the past two years, he had stuck with this one, the Gerer Synagogue, when he went to shul, which was a couple of times a month, anyway. They had grown accustomed to his face, he felt, and they did not begrudge him his attire, which was his Sunday best of slacks, dark socks and shoes, a belt, and a light dress shirt. He prayed at the edges, and if they did not warm to him, they were aware of him, which was much the same thing in these surroundings.

Oscar guessed that no one else coming out of the shul noticed the tall thin black man leaning against the street lamp across Yavne. Oscar waited what must have been three full minutes in stillness while the congregants filed out around him. Then he placed his right hand in his pants pocket and crossed the street.

Pastor Michael Kuur removed his pork-pie hat. "Good

evening, Oscar," he grinned warmly. "I apologize if I am disturbing your evening contemplation. I wish to speak to you. May I walk with you toward your destination, or do you already have company?"

Oscar couldn't help grinning back. It was impossible not to enjoy the thoughtfulness and sincerity Pastor Kuur attached to each component of his greeting. He often missed the unmistakable mix of formality and ease that was so familiar from his youth. Oscar decided in a flash that Kuur's leisurely manner would be a special Saturday evening treat as he walked home. He was grateful for the serendipity.

They turned down Maze toward Allenby. The air was so still that the wind from their moving legs rustled the leaves and a plastic bag stuck at the base of a parking meter. Two cars sat at odd angles on top of the sidewalk. Either could have been assigned to the meter, but it was impossible to tell which, and neither driver would have paid even if it weren't Shabbat. In this country, parking regulations were aspirational. Oscar leaned his hips around the first hood and then the second. In this place of universal army and civil service, of kibbutzim and communitarian dreams, and of European socialist politics, trash piled up where depositors felt moved to leave it, sidewalks were deemed part of the road, and lazy youth copied the graffiti styles of lazy youth in Berlin, who copied the youth of 1980s Berlin, who had copied the youth of 1980s New York. This place of statistically impossible civic cooperation had never forged a lasting culture of civic responsibility. Despite the politics, the Intifada, the police, the Likud, the whatever you could name, the only thing Oscar could bring himself to deplore about Israel was that it was not civilized.

They walked in silence as was their custom, until Kuur felt the mood had been reset and Oscar would be prepared to listen.

"I am afraid I withheld some pertinent information from

Inspector Sambinsky," he began at last. Oscar said nothing and continued to walk as before. "The young victim Kinga: there was another like him eight years ago in Tel Aviv."

Oscar's chin shot up in attention. "Toposa?" he asked.

"He was in fact a Toposa," Kuur nodded solemnly.

"What happened to him?"

"He disappeared after a couple of months. Perhaps he went on to Europe, or perhaps he went back."

"Or maybe he died."

"Perhaps. But Oscar, that is not the all of it. This young man of some years ago bore several further resemblances to the unfortunate fellow discovered this morning. He also exhibited tribal scarring save on his arms."

"How do you know that?"

"I have had some hours to refresh my recollection with friends in the community who saw him bathing."

"And what else?"

"They looked alike, to my eyes, at least. Though perhaps that much is not unlikely given the size of their tribe and my unfamiliarity with their features."

"And what else?"

"He called himself Kinga."

Oscar stopped. He put his hands on his hips and looked at his shoes. The murmur of voices enjoying Sunday night on Yishkon next to the Shuk Ha'Carmel could be heard over the intervening rooftops. Here on Malan they were alone except for a young couple dressed like Americans heading for dinner.

"I apologize, Oscar. I did not want to tell you in front of the police. In case."

"In case what?"

"I do not know, Oscar. They are not us."

After a minute, Oscar started walking again. "What else can you tell me?"

"I regret, Oscar, that this is all I can impart."

They walked another block in silence along Malan. Streetlamps cast sallow light on the cars and mopeds, and, in front of a market, stacks of empty fruit crates. An Abyssinian cat sniffed at a mini Coke can and looked up with bright yellow eyes as they passed. Oscar knew that, in spite of the finality of Kuur's last statement, the pastor was waiting for him to say goodnight. To impose so suddenly as he had on Oscar's evening and then to take leave abruptly without permission would be too vulgar. Oscar weighed another delicate question as they ambled. He watched the cat follow him with her gaze and considered how flimsy it would be if he took the glowing golden color emerging from her irises as a sign of what he should do.

"Michael." He decided to commit. "The coroner discovered a nugget of gold in the young man's mouth, concealed in a cavity of one of his back molars." Oscar felt the air stiffen between them. Somehow Pastor Kuur was not altogether surprised. Or was it something else?

"That must have been very painful," he replied quietly.

Oscar gave a low grunt of affirmation, adding the glottal stop to make sure it came across as noncommittal.

"What do the police make of it?" Kuur asked.

"That I do not know, Pastor," Oscar said slowly. "What do you make of it?"

"Poor child." Kuur looked into the middle distance.

"Do you harbor a notion as to why he might have had it?" Oscar felt no easing of the tension in the air. Kuur's muscles were unrelaxed.

A young woman, probably in her late teens, probably on weekend leave from the army, turned a corner and was startled to see two tall black men immediately in front of her. She recovered fast and visibly blushed in embarrassment and walked past them. For the ten thousandth time in his life, Oscar measured his own instant admixture of forgiveness, desperation, understanding, and anger. He noticed Michael Kuur had barely noticed her, let alone her reaction.

"Perhaps I can ask it another way. Was the young man calling himself Kinga rumored to have visited anyone particularly noteworthy after arriving in Tel Aviv?" He looked directly at Kuur's face. Oscar felt the pause was too long.

"I shall make inquiries immediately. May I telephone you, Oscar?"

"Yes, Michael. Thank you for walking with me. Goodnight."

Kuur stopped, shook hands, and retraced their steps back up the hill.

SIX

I t was not until Monday that Oscar received a phone call, and he received two. The first was from Pastor Michael Kuur in the late morning, and the second from Mefake'ah Sambinsky in the early evening.

Sunday was spent as it often was. In the morning he filled out forms at City Hall on Ibn Gabirol Street, the Brutalist mistake from the thankfully past era of 1950s architectural misunderstanding. Oscar much preferred the old one on Skura Street, the Bauhaus example edging Bialik Square, which was now a museum. That one had the broad white surfaces, long windows, and suggestions of terraces and colonnades apt for the Mediterranean setting. Tel Aviv's designation by UNESCO as the White City – perhaps the only uncontroversial interaction in history between Israel and the United Nations – was based on its collection of four thousand examples of the style, built by European Zionists who made aliyah in the first half of the twentieth century, while Central Europe grew dark for Jewry. The old city hall was the most excellent example of all. But Oscar did not spend time there. Instead, he was often to be found in the city's newer and forsakenly horrible edifice of drab municipal bureaucracy. By now he knew the civil servants in the departments relevant to refugees, and he liked them. They did their work, and they were human beings, and they were compassionate enough, and they were not corrupt. But it made him glum to enter the building. It would have made Mary Poppins glum. By contrast, his social services clients – whom he registered for electricity services, water services, and basic health and education – usually thought it was quite wonderful to be in a large, air conditioned government building where no one was even covertly seeking a gratuity.

At lunchtime, Oscar went to the David Intercontinental to visit with a delegation of American and Canadian Jews who were on a Zionist tour. He told his story, as he often did, and the history of Christian Dinka tribesmen enslaved by Arabs in Sudan, and the allure of Israel for Africans. He understood this group to be largely politically progressive, so he added more grayscale to the narrative of being a refugee today in the country of their forebears, and he added highlights from his own observations of Israelis who had shown compassion to Palestinians, Israeli Arabs, and Syrians. And, as usual, he acknowledged repeatedly how "complicated" – using exactly that word – the felt experiences and human politics were in Israel, "on the ground." All of this endeared him to the audience, who lingered to speak with him on the terrace, next to the pool, across the street and in full view of the Dolphinarium, which Oscar was conscious of eyeing at intervals far, far more frequent than he could have anticipated.

"Oscar, I am calling to follow up with you on the inquiries I promised to make about the young man calling himself Kinga," Kuur said following the customary phone greetings.

"The second one."

"Pardon?"

"The second young man who called himself Kinga. The first one was some years ago."

"Yes, that is correct, Oscar. The second one is of course the young man to whom I refer."

"What did you learn?"

"I believe the young man may have sought contact with Ruben Dumanovsky."

Oscar noticed himself pause longer than he liked to do on the phone. Pauses during mobile calls, unlike in person, were usually meaningless or worse, which meant they were inevitably probably rude. He winced.

"Ruben Dumanovsky? Did I hear you well?" he asked eventually.

"Yes, that is correct."

Oscar knew what it felt like to fear for his life. He had had the sensation before, but so rarely since arriving in Israel that he could count the occasions one by one. It came upon him fast. There instantaneously appeared the very manifest possibility that he would soon come into direct contact with an Israeli businessman known as much for his reputation as a brutal enforcer of contracts he believed he had entered as for his wealth. Twenty years ago, Ruben had arrived from the mists of the Yeltsin disorder. Over time he had advanced various backstories, including Moscow and St. Petersburg, but the general suspicion was that he hailed from Krasnodar Krai or North Caucasus or simply, as some said, from Yerevan. He was not heard to speak Armenian, but he had been observed to be present in small groups when others did. Like many immigrants from that time, he claimed Jewish ancestry. Like some, he was probably of one hundred percent Armenian Orthodox extraction. Or Cossack or just plain Russian Viking. He had arrived penniless, but his education in civil engineering won him work. In time, he purchased economic interests in the construction projects, and soon he had his own concern. No one knew what first moved him to crime. It could have been his ambition to grab more business, or it could have been a competitor who muscled him so he had been forced to push back. But at thirty or thirty-two, he had become a criminal and, eventually, an extremely violent criminal. Some ten years ago, his fortunes had scaled rapidly. Like other Soviet gangsters, he prioritized staying out of the papers, but Israel was a small country with a combative press and a pugnacious citizenry armed with the deepest penetration of social media and the largest number of law degrees in the world, so his accumulation of wealth and upgrades in lifestyle gained attention. Occasionally Oscar would see a photo of Ruben on some site or another, and on occasion the photo would show him sporting a yarmulke. As if he were a real Jew. Then Oscar heard himself think that and sighed. What did that make him?

"Do you know if he made contact with Dumanovsky?"

"I do not. I have been informed only that he was looking to do so."

"And you have no idea why he would know Dumanovsky's name, let alone want to make contact with him?"

"One need not be special liaison to the detective force to make a surmise," Kuur said drily.

To be sure, he is right, Oscar thought. Then he said aloud, after thinking through the possible frailties of translation: "Michael, can you clarify? You believe the young man Kinga was seeking out Ruben Dumanovsky, or you believe Ruben Dumanovsky was trying to find him?"

"Perhaps neither, in fact, Oscar. The more precise way of saying it is that the young man Kinga let it be known that he expected to make contact – or to have contact, I can say – with Mr. Ruben Dumanovsky."

"That could imply that he did not make contact with him," Oscar speculated.

"A meritorious supposition," Pastor Kuur replied, "excepting the fact that he was shot to death in town a fortnight after his arrival."

Oscar felt like an idiot. Then something – a thought flashed through his head. Something he'd heard Kuur say...? He couldn't place it.

The second call came later.

"Oscar, it's me."

The first satisfyingly scalding sip of his evening Americano had just drifted into the back of his throat. La Mer beach bar was without pareil throughout the twenty-four hours of the day, excluding 11 a.m. to 3:30 p.m. in the warm months, when exposure and heat overtook it, and 10 a.m. to 6 p.m. on Shabbat, when the throng did.

"I know it's you, Inspector. I have your number in my mobile." That transitional generation who, out of habit or courtesy, still introduced themselves when they called. For some reason they didn't do it on WhatsApp.

"I've traced the gold. It's from South Sudan."

"You can do that?"

"Yes. If it isn't chemically refined."

"Which it would not be, if it was from Sudan."

"*Nachon.*" *Right.* "It tells us that the victim had brought the gold with him, rather than having been given it after his arrival in Israel."

Oscar nodded in assent. He had learned the manner in detection of stating incremental conclusions based on new evidence. The conclusions were usually quite modest and actually obvious. But something about articulating them collected the efforts of the group and focused his own mind. It was a pattern well captured by the Scandinavian police procedurals to which, like Sambinsky, Oscar was addicted. Until he had experienced it directly, he had found those paragraphs improbable and annoying.

"There is something else," Mefake'ah Sambinsky continued. "We put his face into the system. There is no recording of his having crossed the border, but we have a bunch of hits on CCTV. He was all over Allenby. In the good section."

That was pretty much where Oscar and Kuur had been the other night. It was also...

"Little Russia," Sambinsky said.

The Tel Aviv ex-Soviet community congregated at a Russian language bookstore on the grand Allenby Street called Don Quixote – there, and, for reasons lost to time, at an Irish pub called Molly Bloom's some two kilometers away on Mendele Street. In Oscar's estimation, those two facts were all you needed to know about their level of national confusion.

In any case, Allenby was ground zero. Even for gangsters, who, in inverse proportion to their significance, profiled among the restaurants and cafés and even bookshelves, and upstairs in their apartments and legitimate-ish businesses.

"That makes sense. I have something to tell you, Inspector."

"*Nu?*"

"Pastor Michael Kuur has alerted me that the victim was heard to be in the process of making some form of contact with Ruben Dumanovsky. It is unknown if he did."

"What else did he tell you?" Oscar noticed Sambinsky's voice become serious. This was suddenly the kind of murder case in which police might also die.

"He told me there was another young man, a Toposa, as well, some eight years ago, here in Tel Aviv, who also called himself Kinga and who disappeared after some brief time, and that the two young Kingas seem to have looked alike, including the unusual absence of tribal scarring on their arms."

"Holy shit."

"Very. And I happen to think the righteous Pastor Kuur hasn't yet revealed all that he knows."

"What makes you say that?" Sambinsky sounded very interested.

"Call it a police hunch." Oscar allowed a short cackle. Sambinsky joined him.

"I'll meet you on Allenby at 6:45. Can you do it?" Sambinsky asked.

"You want to go see Dumanovsky?" Oscar felt a flash of adrenaline.

"What else?"

"I have a translation job." Oscar scanned himself. To his surprise, despite the instant fear, his schedule conflict was his authentic first concern.

"I'll pay the normal rates."

"If I can find a substitute... " Oscar knew he could, but it was his way to commit only conditionally until he had done so.

SEVEN

Sambinsky was waiting in an unmarked Honda on the corner of Gruzenberg and Nahalat Binyamin outside a hipster beer and tapas restaurant known for the bicycle placed in its front window. The meeting spot was a block off Allenby and a less conspicuous place for a detective to wait.

Four minutes later, the two men were standing outside a second-floor steel office door painted fresh white with black etching that read "Pasternak Design Build Develop." A squat woman in her late fifties or sixties opened and said nothing, immobile.

"We are here to see Mr. Dumanovsky," Sambinsky said, holding up his police identification. She eyeballed him and then Oscar and closed the door slowly. Two minutes later, she opened it again and made room for them to enter. Then she sat down behind a reception desk and made no gesture or movement apart from looking at her computer. Oscar found himself standing in a front office of what seemed to be a three-room suite. There were no sounds apart from the noises coming up from the street. He looked at Sambinsky, whose face gave the impression of a fighter about to enter the ring.

Footsteps announced the arrival of Ruben Dumanovsky, who opened a door and paused to look at his visitors. Paused, Oscar felt, just a moment too long as he observed the African looming in his foyer. Dumanovsky was a cool, poker-faced character, no doubt. Nearly expressionless. But he still looked just a little longer than he had to when he saw Oscar. And Oscar knew that Dumanovsky knew why they were there.

He was short, shouldered, swarthy, and thick set, like a middle-aged Bob Hoskins playing the part of a street tough gone big. He wore dark blue fitted jeans, shiny brown shoes that gave the impression of cowboy boots, a striped dress shirt with an open collar revealing chest hair and a gold chain tucked away under the buttons, and a tailored sports jacket. A yarmulke sat on top of his balding pate. He stood motionless in the door frame. Tel Aviv's warm sunlight glowed through the front windows and backlit his body. For a second, Oscar was aware that this interlude was probably common to all encounters with gangsters: the home team and the visitors were instantly gauging who would win in unannounced mortal combat. It was ridiculous and frightening.

"You wanted to see me?" Dumanovsky entered the room but kept his distance and made no indication to shake hands.

"I am Mefake'ah Sambinsky of the Israel Police, Tel Aviv District." He presented his ID. "This is my colleague." Oscar was grateful Kobi had not revealed his name but also knew the gesture at privacy was pointless. This criminal could find him in a day. In fact, a half-blind geriatric could. There was exactly one person who looked like Oscar in the city, and that was Oscar. "We are investigating the disappearance of a young immigrant who may have had contact with you recently." Sambinsky stopped to let it sink in. Dumanovsky gave no reaction and continued to stand, square, in the middle of the room. Oscar was aware the receptionist had also not reacted.

"Have you seen this man?" Sambinsky held up a printed photo, enlarged from a street camera, showing the victim Kinga's face. Dumanovsky looked at it for less than a second.

"I meet many people. Many immigrants look for work in construction."

"You would remember him. Very tall, skinny, African."

"I cannot help you." Dumanovsky moved so little it seemed he might not have the physiological need to blink. Oscar hated every moment of this. Violence was apparent in each second and syllable. He wondered fleetingly of the life he could have had as an economist in the ministry of his home country, or at the World Bank. If only violence had not killed that dream.

"I see. Then we are perhaps finished here," the Inspector said slowly. "Please tell me: where were you last night?"

"I was at home," Dumanovsky replied, after a brief pause that Oscar would have guessed was intentional, as if to signal he was not overly relieved to have a ready alibi. "With my family."

"Thank you. Well, if you see him, or if you remember anything, please call me right away." Sambinsky deposited his card on the receptionist's desk. She didn't move her eyes from her computer.

Sambinsky turned, as did Oscar to follow him, and then the detective stopped at the door and did the Columbo thing Oscar had seen him do a hundred times before. "You are sure you never met him?" he asked. "You see, we have many images of him from CCTV walking several times within meters of this office just a couple of days ago, and we understand from witnesses that he has been in contact with you."

"There are many attractive shops and cafés downstairs," Dumanovsky answered drily. "Perhaps if you tell me his name, I can ask my colleagues if they met him. Most of them have gone home for the day."

"Well, in case you remember," Sambinsky answered. "You see, there is some cause for alarm. It seems this young man has been walking around town with some amount of pure gold on his person." Oscar swore he saw Dumanovsky's chest rise just barely for the first time. The receptionist looked up. Sambinsky continued. "Perhaps you share an interest in gold, from what I have heard. But no doubt you also share our concern that such a recent arrival, toting pure gold around, unfamiliar with the city, not meet with any unexpected harm." He smiled at Dumanovsky and, without waiting for an answer, walked out.

"If that squat sack of shit is a Jew, I am Hermann Goering," he said as he sat back into the driver seat of his Honda. Always the Holocaust jokes, Oscar thought to himself. His heart fluttered for what was probably the millionth time at the marvelous resilience of this tiny people, who made life out of even that infinity of death.

"I take it I was not alone in having the impression that he knew exactly who Kinga was."

"No, you were not, detective," Sambinsky replied. "Cool as ice, that Russian Armenian shitbag. More to the point, he knows we have no fucking clue who the guy actually was. Asking me for his name... Smug shitdrain."

"You suspect him of involvement in the young man's death?"

Sambinsky tapped the steering wheel rhythmically. "I don't know. I don't know. But I do know that fuckstick is an archcriminal. He could kill a poor bastard, and his breakfast wouldn't taste any different."

EIGHT

Twenty years ago, after the army, Mefake'ah Sambinsky had backpacked by himself to Japan. His friends had wanted to do the world tour, with lingering focus on Thailand, Chile, and other countries known to be friendly to Jews and kids on tight budgets. But for reasons he could no longer cite – and probably for a reason no more intelligent than that a guy he had met in a bar when he was twenty had talked about it – he had determined to make the Shikoku Pilgrimage as soon as he was discharged from the army.

Eighty-eight temples over twelve hundred kilometers had given him no enlightenment. But the walking had made him love Japan. Excluding short trips in a Merkava tank, it was his first voyage outside Israel, and the place had invaded him. He remained in Japan for eight months, nearly the entirety of his time abroad, leaving only a few weeks for Los Angeles, Las Vegas, and then New York.

He had stayed long enough to meet a girl, Kanako, in Kyoto, at the bar next to the hostel, and to date her and even, for a month at the end, to find himself living in her eleven-square-meter room, with a washbasin and hotplate, where they had to share her one set of dishes. Their lives were separated from her roommates' by the thinnest walls he had ever touched and a sliding door that was made out of faux rice paper. The room was stiflingly hot, cooked by the abutting shared kitchen stove, the landlady's reluctance to turn off the steam radiator lest it cease working, and the closeness of their bodies. Only the bedroom's scuttle-sized casement window allowed them to cool off. But the window gave partially onto the river – and completely if you leaned out to smoke cigarettes – and Kanako's skin and small body gave him all the happiness he needed. His Japanese was tiny, her Hebrew smaller, and their English hardly better. But they were in love, and he had never since felt as much passion in his life.

When Kobi had left Japan, it was suddenly, and for the exact reasons a young Jewish boy might flee a puppy romance with a waitress in a distant land. He had longed to return ever since a few days after his departure. But he had not yet done so. He was afraid that, should he go, he would finally be faced with learning if she had in fact been pregnant and if she had kept the baby. Almost every time he had thought of her, which he estimated to be daily, he had hoped she had been and did, and that one day he would meet the child of his young love.

For nearly three decades, he had managed his passions by owning a succession of Akita dogs. In his own small way, he had become ground zero of pure-bred Akita culture in Israel. There were only three Akita Ken hounds in the country when he had started, and there were only a few dozen now. The Japanese mountain dog had little business living in a Mediterranean climate. But he loved them because they were Japanese and because they and their Japanese-ness were his. Akita ownership had become the only public part of his private identity. It was his way of socializing his devotion to a chapter in his life without revealing too much. His friends, such as he had them, didn't really have to ask why he didn't return to Japan. It was enough for them to imagine his policeman's salary and wife's xenophobia were the probable reasons.

Kobi could sit late at night on his JFK rocking chair, an inheritance from his father who had admired the man for reasons his son had never quite asked, place his feet into L. L. Bean Wicked Good sheepskin slippers, the linings of which were a close enough match for his Akitas' fur, and rub his dog's head and imagine he was somewhere cold, in the presence of a still youthful Kanako, in the midst of his other life.

Tonight he was dozing off in his chair, as he usually did these days, awaiting the signal on his mobile phone. On nights his son Itai sent him a text between 9 p.m. and midnight, he would keep vigil in the chair until he received the second one between 1 a.m. and dawn. A "1" to indicate he was going on patrol or some other operation, and a "2" to say he was safely returned. Itai Sambinsky, their only child, was *tzanchan*, a paratrooper. Now, at twenty-two, he was an officer. Kobi suspected he was in a secret unit; he was too often on maneuvers not to be. Without admitting anything, Itai had agreed to notify his father when he was out and when he was back, so Kobi would not worry needlessly. They had concurred it would not do to tell his mother anything about it, as she would never have slept. Itai was the only thing Kobi and his wife deeply shared. About him, they agreed on everything. Itai wished to study physics after the army at Ben Gurion University in the Negev. Automatically, this had struck his parents as a brilliant idea. By now, Kobi knew the names and pedigrees of every professor there, though he had never visited.

At 2:22 a.m., his phone buzzed in his hand and woke him. He looked, saw the "2," and ambled to the bedroom, where his wife was snoring. *Sheleg*, Snow, the mother of his three dog family, knew the routine as well as he did and had waited up with him till they'd heard from Itai. She followed him to bed and lay down next to his night table.

NINE

On the other side of town, Oscar Orleans sat ramrod straight, his right hand resting on the external mouse of his laptop. He had decided upon moving into the flat that he would keep the surface area of his one and only table clear and spare-looking so that with each use it could feel fresh. At university, he had acted in one play and written two. None of it had been very good, but his writing, at least, had won him admirers for his revolutionary sensibility. And enemies. It was in university theater that he had learned how minor adjustments could make for a visible "set change" on stage. He had applied that observation to his life in this small flat. If he was to live in such a tiny space, on what was perhaps the tiniest street in all Tel Aviv, he would at least create the impression for himself of having more rooms by visibly altering the function when the occasion arose. Breakfast at home was a plate and utensils and a flower in his only vase. Lunch and dinner were the same with a basket for bread and a napkin covering it, whether or not there was bread. No computer of any kind was allowed during meals. Though he lived alone – perhaps because he lived alone – his hat-tip to his own mental health was to make an emphatic if arbitrary rule that, at mealtime, he would not even read the newspaper on a screen. This meant he had to read the actual newspaper, which he could scarcely afford, so he made it a habit to read yesterday's, which he picked up from a downstairs neighbor's discard pile most evenings when he came home. For work, he would remove the placemat and situate the laptop, a sleek Acer Chromebook in perfect condition, in the same spot. His mouse pad and mouse on the right, a notepad or a sheaf of papers or a book on the left, and the glass of water or other on the windowsill just above the table so it wouldn't spill on the computer. His practice was to stay erect at the table until he grew too tired and only then allow himself to slump casually in his chair or put his bare feet up under the table onto the opposite one. Now it was after 11 p.m., and he was starting to feel the need to slump. The small of his back was hurting.

As it was a weekday, the music from the nearby bars would start to fade soon. It was not so bad here on Simtat Neve Tzedek. Tucked behind Shabazi, the *Simtah*, the Alley, was blocked from the main sources of late night noise that dominated his little, fashionable neighborhood by the front-facing buildings, which acted as baffles. If Shabazi had become some of the priciest real estate in the city over the past decade, his miniscule elbow-shaped Simtat Neve Tzedek, only meters away, had remained an unrepentant decrepit backwater from the 1970s. Oscar occupied the flat on the back side of an odd bookstore that styled itself a gathering place for Tel Aviv's literary and artistic cognoscenti. Four years ago, he had seen a poster for an evening launch of a book about the history of communist agitprop art in the Third World. He had attended, for a change of scene as much as for any other reason.

He had enjoyed himself immensely at the talk, and he had stayed afterwards to linger in the companionship of educated people and to drink a second glass of very good red wine from the Galilee. Perhaps elated by the wine and the setting, he had found himself speaking with the author about his own experience as a youth rehearsing secondary school plays that had been written during the height of Congo's communist era. An older woman, her grey hair bundled high above her head, dressed in a black utility jumpsuit and a massive Yemenite silver necklace, had joined them. The evening wore on, and Oscar realized they were the last three to remain in the store. Feeling embarrassed, he had begun to take his leave when the two women grabbed his arms and ferried him across the street to a wine bar, where they had remained till the early hours.

The evening had been a breath of new life. The older woman, named Hannah Huchler, turned out to be the proprietor of the Simple Stories bookstore. She asked him for his mobile number before the night ended, and she soon called to invite him to come to another event, this time a book launch by a music critic. It took a full month of such invitations and then a lunch and then a coffee for him to accept that she was not seeking a romantic attachment and that she was motivated only very partly by a guilty or hedonistic desire to affiliate herself with an educated African. He told her about his childhood, his university days, his flight from Congo, his journey overland, his life here, his accidental calling of assisting other Africans with the navigation of the social and immigration services, his path toward Judaism, and his dream to be part of this country. One afternoon, she plucked a set of keys off the wall of her store, walked him outside and around the back of the building, up a flight of narrow stainless steel stairs, and through a door that did not sit easily on its hinges. The flat was small, unpainted, and covered in dust.

"Yours, until my son comes home," she had declared, handing him the keys. "You can use the bookstore Wi-Fi. It reaches here, mostly. You pay the hot water, you clean it up, you help with the trash, and you don't owe me anything. *Nachon?"* *Right? Agreed?*

She had left before he could say anything, and he was humbled and grateful that she had understood so well that, had she done it any other way, he would have felt obligated to refuse her kindness.

For more than three years, he had made this place his home. The space was tiny but no tinier, really, than what he had had before, and it was far less crowded. Almost no one else lived on the Alley, and there were no Africans for almost half a kilometer. At first he would wince at that thought. But he had come to accept that a measure of privacy was praiseworthy, and for good and ill reasons he had less of it in South Tel Aviv and more of it here.

Oscar had spent the evening preparing for the meeting with his lawyer Tamar Ben Artzi. Tamar was a central casting Israeli social justice attorney. Educated at Hebrew University and Harvard Law School for her L.L.M., she was also an alumna of Unit 8200, the fearsome signals intelligence department and one of the country's most elite warfare branches. Both her parents had been officers, her father rising to the rank of general before meeting with a terrible car accident that had led to a nearly permanent state of disability. One of her brothers had staked out the unique family dissident role as refusenik, which meant, in his case, that he refused to serve in units that would be involved in the occupation of Palestinian territories. Tamar had, in contrast, vigorously embraced her intelligence role in the Israel Defense Forces, but then, in energetic sympathy or similarity, had chosen a path of progressive social cause work in her legal career. As Tamar had explained to Oscar before inviting him to Shabbat dinner a year ago, everyone at the table would be simultaneously resentful and proud of one another.

He had sat mostly silently and marveled at the thrilling speed of the clashes and rapprochements among the parents and four children and two spouses and three grandkids. He could not have imagined a more different dining experience than the one he had grown up with, which was alternately silent or joyful but always, in one manner or another, austere. His father – that patriarch – a single move of a muscle or the slightest word from his lips, and... oh, how the family would jump and swoon. Oscar smiled to himself and then grew sad, aware of the distance, of the absence, of the funeral he had missed.

Apart from a terrific set of hips, which Oscar usually endeavored not to notice, Tamar had one of the largest heads and heads of hair he had ever encountered in his life. Mounds of curly, dark brown mane tumbled from her enormous crown, and her eyes and face flashed her brilliance several times per minute and every time she had a new thought, which was nearly as often. He had first met her some years ago when she was a fresh lawyer assigned to a Sudanese refugee family whom he'd been helping. He had noticed immediately her rookie ignorance of basic procedural items as well as the misplaced undifferentiated emphasis on every question she came across that was so typical of first-year lawyers. But he was also struck with her zeal, and he was especially struck when he realized, a year later, that her zeal had not abated but had instead grown. She had also accumulated a modest conversational level of Dinka to accompany a flawless English and what Oscar had gathered, from no more than five minutes of overheard conversation across twelve months, was an unaccented Arabic. As he watched the first cases she handled unfold, he compared her to his own immigration lawyer, a bright and experienced if unenthusiastic veteran named Omri, and he came to envy the Sudanese families Tamar was assisting.

After a week of wrestling with the decision and another of practicing how to make the request, he asked her to become his lawyer. It was his greatest act of bravery and self-interest since he had fled Kinshasa.

For three hours now he had been updating his file in advance of his consultation with her in the morning. It was a night of collating. He reviewed the case files of his refugee clients and typed into the laptop the services he had provided. He noted the talks he had given to Zionist tour groups. He wrote a précis of an op-ed he had published in the *Jerusalem Post*. Anything to explain how he had been contributing to the Jewish state since he had last met with her two months earlier. He also added his attendance at shul. Tamar would read these notes about his religious practice and assure him, as she always had, that it wasn't material and wouldn't help. But he added it anyway, as he believed it would. He was part of the community, he was ensconced, he was active. He wanted that to come across.

Oscar's immigration case had bounced around the civil service for twenty years. In that time, the law of Israel had evolved. When he had first arrived, there had been virtually no provision for admitting or rejecting people who were neither Jews, nor Arabs, nor clerics. Certainly not African refugees. It just hadn't come up much. No one in the world had really wanted to come to Israel. There had been little economic reason for non-Jewish asylum seekers to immigrate, and there had been almost no way for them physically to reach Israel's borders. The world had changed, as had Israel's fortunes, and it had become a destination. The law had followed.

Nowadays, the Population and Immigration Authority and Refugee Status Determination Unit of the Ministry of the Interior were in charge. Tamar was employed by the same, as were a cadre of other government lawyers with dedicated or mixed-department responsibility, among them the erstwhile Omri.

And two decades on, Oscar was still here, still in Israel, the only country he had known apart from his home, and, after all this time, what was the difference? His asylum application was inching on at a glacial pace. Tomorrow would be just another day, briefing his lawyer so she could keep tapping at it for him.

Oscar looked at the open file on his computer one last time and clicked to share it with the huge-headed, beatific-hipped Tamar. He noticed he was slouching in his chair and laughed at himself. Standing, he closed his laptop, put away the mouse and paper and refreshment from the windowsill and replaced the placemat. Then, opening the window fully and switching on the fan, he placed his heavy glass ashtray on the outdoor ledge and, with the formality of a waiter he had seen in the movie *Casablanca*, set down an aluminum packet of Ashton Esquires and a tumbler in the middle of the mat and poured one finger of Havana Club 7. Then he pulled out his chair, sat carefully with one knee over the other, raised his glass to the middle of the room, and sipped.

TEN

Oscar smiled into the September sun. Tamar had been as efficient and intelligent as ever. She had digested the documented updates before their appointment, and she had walked him through the current status of his application, which was an appeal on the technical question whether Oscar's earlier lawyer had timely provided the mandated episodic memorandum on the political state of play in Congo and whether conditions had sufficiently changed for an asylum seeker – specifically, this asylum seeker – to return. She reiterated that it was not a matter of utmost importance, for Oscar's main application had transitioned from one of simple asylum seeking to one of permanent residency, but a ruling about missing portions of his file could have the effect of delaying, for another six months easily, any forward motion on his core submission. Of course, in a matter of trying to stay in a country, the value of six months' delay could cut both ways.

Oscar strode down Jerusalem's Queen Shlomziyon Street away from the Population and Immigration Authority with a little extra lightness in his step. Meeting with Tamar was always so... life affirming. She was energetic, strong, knowledgeable, and confidence-building. What else could one want from one's closest life counselor? There was nothing to do except keep living his life. At least he was here, in Israel, on this boulevard, and not in Congo or Sudan or Yemen or Saudi or Zimbabwe or any of the other places he might have been, could have been, but for the grace of a loving G–d. He said the Shehecheyanu, the Jewish prayer for the moment, out loud.

Baruch atah Adonai elohenu melech ha'olam, shehecheyanu, vekiymanu, vehigi'anu lazman hazeh.

Blessed are You, Lord our G–d, King of the Universe, who has granted us life, sustained us, and enabled us to reach this day.

He looked at his phone. Kobi had called once and sent him a text "call me" at 10:54 a.m. It was now 11:40, and there had been no follow up, so it did not seem urgent, at least from Sambinsky's point of view. But something about it felt urgent to Oscar. Ever since leaving Dumanovsky's office, he had sensed the spirit of violence overhanging him, a kind of terror that he could not yet ascribe to facts or to his brain's working overtime.

"Hello, Oscar." Sambinsky picked up after one ring. "How was your morning?"

Oscar felt relieved at once. Mefake'ah Sambinsky was cordial in this way only when he'd had some form of good news, like the appearance of a new clue or the confirmation of a hunch. Oscar had never known the detective to ask a polite personal question in a moment of crisis.

"I've had a very agreeable morning, thank you, Inspector. How was yours?" Oscar asked, knowing there was slim chance of getting an answer.

"Border patrol has no record of anyone immigrating with the

face of the victim," Sambinsky continued, sounding almost elated.

"Yes, I remember," Oscar reported.

"But! But! There is a hit on the database of someone with the name Kinga."

"Really?" Oscar stopped walking on the street and heard himself yelp. "That is *very* interesting."

"Twelve years ago."

"Twelve years ago?"

"Exactly. Name of Kinga Longokwo."

"*Sapristi! Zela!*" *Heavens! Wait!* Even after two decades, in moments of actual surprise, Oscar still fell back on the exclamations of his youth, largely a combination of his own Lingala and of the antique colonial French that remained the official language of Congo. Much of the vocabulary of youthful astonishment in his home country was sourced, quite directly, from the pages of Tintin's adventures. "Kinga Longokwo, you said? As in Father Kinga Longokwo? He was here? In Eretz Israel?"

"In Eretz Israel itself, himself. The self-same one, from Sudan. He came here for three weeks with a delegation of East African clergymen and flew out on schedule back to Addis Ababa."

"Why was he here?"

"I don't know. You did say he was a Catholic priest. Probably the group was here for a pilgrimage."

"Yes, yes, no doubt they would have toured the holy places." Oscar sensed himself mouthing the words without endowing them with too much meaning. One advantage of habitual politeness was, as Alice had learned in Wonderland, that it gave you time to think. He rubbed the outside of his left eye with the back of his thumb. "And yet... "

"*Nachon meod.*" *Exactly right.* "Our friend Pastor Kuur hasn't been telling us the whole story."

"I am afraid I must concur with your assessment."

"What is the chance that Father Kinga Longokwo, a national figure in South Sudan, visited Israel in the middle of the refugee swell and did not interact with Michael Kuur?"

"It is unlikely. He must have met him."

"Then it's time to go back to see Kuur and find out what else he knows and why he has been withholding information from us. Do you want to come?"

"Yes, I do. I am this morning in Jerusalem, but I can take a bus back and be there in maybe ninety minutes."

"Send me a WhatsApp when you know when you're arriving, and I'll meet you at the station. It will be faster."

ELEVEN

Just after 1:30 p.m., Sambinsky parked his Honda on Neve Sha'anan Street just outside Jebena, Pastor Michael Kuur's so-called private club. The door swung open, but traffic inside seemed very light. An elderly lady was sitting against the back wall minding a small stove on which guhwah brewed fragrantly. Apparently no one else was about.

Kobi looked at Oscar, who nodded and stepped forward to place himself in front of the detective.

"Madame, good afternoon," Oscar began in Dinka. "We are searching for Pastor Kuur. Do you know where he might be?"

The lady waved her hand. "He is not here. Not here." She returned her attention to the pot and gave it a stir. Undoubtedly an excellent cup of guhwah was on its way to one mouth or another. Oscar salivated.

"Do you know when he might return, Madame?" Oscar bowed again.

"Not here, not here," she waved once more. Oscar looked at Kobi, who clearly required no interpretation. Old, reluctant ladies looked the same in all languages.

They stepped outside.

"Do you know where he lives?" Sambinsky asked.

"Just up the road. If he is still in the same place." Oscar would have been surprised if Kuur had moved. Almost no Sudanese ever moved in Tel Aviv. On every level, such a move would be difficult to pull off.

Two blocks away sat HaGalil Street, even more derelict than Neve Sha'anan. Every building was two stories, and nearly every storefront was empty, disused for what could have been eternity. A single tree was to be found along the entire thoroughfare. Telephone and electrical wires were strung from poles to houses and back to poles. The sun beat down on the unsheltered pavement and cinderblock.

Above the boarded and plastered windows on street level, there was the impression of life on the second floors. External air conditioners hummed. Those were probably offices of startups, Oscar thought. In others, window curtains fluttered from wind presumably blown by electric fans. Those would be residences. Mostly immigrants, one or two startup founders, and maybe the odd rabbinical student. The hip set would never live here. It was too shitty.

Oscar led the way up an unsteady external staircase and knocked on a well-maintained door. Someone had painted it in the black, red, white, and green of the 2005 flag of South Sudan and had even taken care to paint the blue hoist side triangle and gold star. The colors were unfaded, which meant, in this neighborhood with such limited outdoor shade, they were frequently and lovingly refreshed.

A young woman, maybe twenty or twenty-five, opened the door. Oscar was taken aback by her flourishing beauty. Close-cropped hair, perfectly proportionate features, dark, unblemished skin. She wore long green earrings and a matching dress speckled with gold. A massive necklace sprawled across her clavicle and down to the middle of her sternum. Her face was square, less typical of her people than a long visage, but it worked for her. For all her beauty, a look of sadness lay across her countenance. Oscar reflexively removed his hat.

"Mademoiselle, my name is Oscar Orleans. I am acquainted with the Pastor Michael Alou Kuur Kuur. I have some business with him. May I inquire as to whether he is at home?"

She hesitated, and he realized she was looking past him.

"Oh, I do apologize. This is my colleague Inspector Kobi Sambinsky of the Israel Police, Tel Aviv District." Sambinsky, standing three steps lower on the staircase, gave a half smile.

"Yes, my husband is at home," she replied in English. As she spoke, she looked down, perhaps as a show of modesty. "I am glad you have come. You are welcome here. I did not know if the police would do anything."

Oscar's heart fluttered. An abundance of new information had flooded him all at once, which was often the way with new information. Pastor Kuur was married. To a stunning Dinka woman. Who was educated enough to converse easily in English.

And savvy enough to choose English so that the Israeli police officer behind him might understand her. To boot, something inside the dwelling was already off. She had been half expecting, half wanting the police to arrive for reasons unknown to him and Sambinsky but clearly known to her.

She made way for them to enter. Observing her shoes were still on, Oscar made no move to remove his own. She reached out her hand for his hat, and he gladly offered it to her.

"Please go in," she said. "I shall bring you both cold water."

Ah, Africa, Oscar thought to himself. Where cold water is a plentiful gesture of hospitality. To be sure, she would appear also with some form of sliced fruit. He led Sambinsky down a short hallway toward what he recalled was the sitting room. The flat had taken a turn for the better since his last visit. The walls featured hangings, the colors were brighter, fabrics touched this and that surface, the lighting was intentional, and the scents were pleasant. Flowers stood in a bouquet on a shelf in the sitting room. A woman's touch had beautified the house.

Michael Kuur sat on a large cushioned chair near the windows. He did not rise when they entered. Oscar could see why. He gasped aloud. He heard Kobi breathe in, too.

The left side of Pastor Kuur's face was covered by a large bandage. His lips were swollen and bloodied. And his left hand was completely wrapped in gauze. Someone had beaten him up, and very badly.

"Michael, are you okay? I can't believe it!" Oscar exclaimed as he approached. He knelt beside the chair and held Kuur's good hand in his.

Sambinsky stood next to him. "Pastor Kuur, do you need assistance? Have you been seen by a doctor?" he asked.

Kuur nodded slowly. It was clear from his expression that even such a small movement gave him pain.

"Are you all right, Pastor?" Oscar came again.

Kuur raised his hand to indicate that they should sit on the couch across from him. They did. It was a small sofa, for two, not built for a pair of grown men.

"I am afraid my accommodation is not suitable for visitors of your stature," Kuur said, his words coming as a slur from the side of his mouth. He laughed at his own pun, and then he coughed, which seized his face like a back-handed slap.

Kobi and Oscar both offered up a short cackle to compliment Kuur on his humor and on the manliness of his implied disregard for his own injuries.

The lady of the house entered with a tray. Two glasses of water perspired with evidence of their coldness, and slices of melon lay on a blue and white plate. She set the refreshments before them.

"You must conserve your strength," she said softly to her husband. Then she sat on a wooden chair facing both Kuur and the visitors. Oscar was sure even Kobi would be aware that this gesture of joining the conversation was a statement in itself.

"What happened?" Oscar asked after sipping the water and indicating both thanks and a sensation of relief. He and Kobi stared at Kuur, awaiting an answer. Kuur stared back, and then to the middle distance, looking confused. Oscar felt he must be feigning. Kobi said nothing. They turned to the woman, who looked worried. She shifted in her chair and bit her lip. Then it looked as if she might say something, and the visitors instinctively remained motionless, aware of the fragility of the moment.

Apparently, Pastor Kuur was aware, too.

"Tired," he said loudly, uttering a sentence fragment for the first time Oscar could ever recall. He gestured toward his head. "Hurts."

A baby's cry emerged from the back hallway. Oscar and Kobi looked up and found each other giving the same automatic unaffected smile one gives when suddenly becoming aware of newborn life. Their hostess cocked her head to listen, grinned, and then resumed her pose as she realized the cry was fleeting.

"I did not realize you were a father, Michael! Congratulations!" Oscar said.

"*Mazal tov*," Kobi agreed.

Kuur smiled and winced and murmured a *toda raba* – *thank you very much* – then closed his eyes as if wanting to rest. Oscar could not tell if he was exaggerating his condition.

"Yes, we are very blessed to have a daughter. She is six months old now," his wife said warmly.

"Very sorry to see you are in such pain, Mr. Kuur."

Sambinsky rose. Oscar followed suit. The detective spoke again. "Madame, I am afraid I did not learn your name. Mine is Kobi Sambinsky. Please take my card so you or your husband may reach out when he is feeling better."

"I am so sorry. My name is Lily Kuur." She smiled brilliantly, and Oscar felt himself swoon at the coalescence of sensual and maternal beauty. She was easily one of the most exceptional-looking women he had ever seen. To find such elegance and energy in a second-floor flatlet on seedy old HaGalil Street... He looked away in shame, feeling that he was perhaps gawking like a schoolboy at another man's wife. He could not help being overcome with embarrassment that he was so quickly enraptured by a woman's visage, figure, and grace, and by his imagined understanding of what kind of lady and mother she must be. He had so little information, and yet he was already so delighted by her. *Foolish*, he thought to himself.

Lily smiled. Oscar had averted his eyes too obviously. She had noticed. She bowed her gaze and head toward the floor in a generous show of politeness. The gesture gave Oscar all the time he needed to recover and wonder briefly what it might be like to be in love with such a wondrous woman.

"I shall walk you gentlemen to the door." She stepped to her husband's chair, refreshed a pillow behind his head, and followed them down the hallway. Kobi opened the door. After they had stepped onto the ledge, Oscar turned and looked at her face. She was ready to talk.

"Do you know what happened, Madame Kuur?" he asked. Kobi leaned against the railing to watch her reaction.

"I am afraid I do not. Michael came home badly bruised and bleeding. He would not tell me anything. He was even reluctant to visit the hospital, though of course I prevailed upon him."

Oscar had learned through experience that it was best in

such a moment to wait in stillness. Kobi was so good at it that Oscar could sense his relaxation.

"If you are here – if the police are here... " She trailed off. Then she started again. "If you are here, it must be... bad. Has he met with some serious trouble?" She raised her hand to her mouth, perhaps realizing the ineptitude of her phrasing. "I mean, you see... Now that there is the baby... " She began to tear up, and then managed to recover.

Sambinsky leaned forward from the railing of the staircase landing and showed her the screen of his phone. Oscar could see the photo of a scowling Ruben Dumanovsky in the corner of his eye.

"Do you recognize this man?" Sambinsky asked.

"Yes, yes, I do," Lily stammered. "But I do not remember where I have seen him. Is he responsible for this?" She reduced her voice to a whisper and gestured into the house.

"It is possible," Sambinsky said gravely. "Look again. You are sure you have seen him? Where? Please try to think, Mrs. Kuur."

She closed her eyes. After some time, she shook her head. "I cannot be sure. But I think I recall seeing him outside the Jebena in the back seat of a large motorcar. But perhaps... I mostly saw his profile."

"When, Mrs. Kuur? When did you see him? This is extremely important."

"I think it must have been last week. It was quite recent. On most days, I will take Nellie out for a walk in the afternoon to visit her father at the Jebena."

"Thank you, Mrs. Kuur. You have been very helpful."

Oscar knew enough to know that Lily had almost certainly named her baby after the *Nellie Chapin*, the ship that ferried Tel Aviv's first hopeful American settlers in 1866, before Tel Aviv even existed. A band of Christian fanatics had sailed from Maine, landed near Jaffa, and mostly died of cholera. They brought their own wooden houses with them, which the survivors reconstructed some time after they arrived. A massive cement block along the sea was the main remembrance for them in Israel. That, and a couple of their surviving frame buildings near Neve Tzedek, which one charitable foundation or another had restored in recent decades. For this remarkable lady and her husband, who had no doubt walked these neighborhoods and along the seaside boulevard a thousand times, naming their daughter after the *Nellie Chapin* was a dedication of their family and affection, a love poem to immigration, offered up to a land that inspired in them a passion for G–d and an optimism for their future, expressed in the fact of their daughter. Oscar also knew enough to know something that she did not and could not: what a misapprehension must have given rise to the choice of name, at least as far as Israelis would be concerned, if ever they had occasion to be concerned. Your average Israeli would not know the name *Nellie Chapin* and would scarcely credit the association if he did.

Oscar likewise knew enough to know there was no point in moving from his perch in the doorway. Kobi was about to do his Columbo thing.

"One more question," Sambinsky continued. "I wonder if you ever heard Pastor Kuur mention a fellow man of the cloth. He was called Father Longokwo."

Lily screwed up her face. "No," she said, shaking her head gently. "I do not remember a Father Longokwo."

"Please think carefully. Father Kinga Longokwo."

"Kinga?" She looked surprised. "I met Kinga! I had no idea he is a priest." Her expression indicated something was not making sense to her.

"When did you meet him?" Sambinsky asked, leaning forward.

"He was in our house." She swept her arm back reflexively toward the hallway and living room beyond. "He is so young."

"I think you met someone who shared the name Kinga but was a different figure. Father Longokwo himself died some years back," Sambinsky offered, watching her carefully.

Lily looked relieved. "Oh, that makes sense. You know, I can remember now hearing stories about a Father Longokwo when I was a girl. We are from different tribes. I remember hearing he was a great man in South Sudan. But I cannot remember why."

Sambinsky nodded. "Thank you, Madame. That is enough for today. If you think of anything, please call me." He smiled and turned to go.

"Goodbye, Mrs. Kuur," Oscar said, gripping the rim of his hat more tightly than he had planned. "May I please be allowed to compliment you on your Yemenite necklace. It becomes you greatly, and likewise you do it great justice." He felt his heart pound.

Lily beamed and bowed her head in the manner of a girl perhaps not accustomed to receiving praise. "You are very kind. But it is not Yemenite, Mr. Orleans. It is Sudanese," she said proudly.

"Is it?" he asked.

"Yes! The best traditions of jewelry from the region all come from the Nile River. You must know that, sir." She smiled at him. "The Yemenites must have copied us. This necklace was my dowry. Transporting it to Israel was far easier than bringing cattle." She laughed out loud at her own joke, perhaps even more heartily than she would have otherwise because the tension was now broken. Oscar laughed, too, his hand on his belly. Kobi joined. Then Lily realized she had maybe acknowledged some form of familial smuggling to a policeman, and she covered her mouth. Sambinsky understood and waved his hand to indicate no harm.

"Thank you again for your hospitality," Oscar said. "We must be going."

As they walked back to the car, Oscar waited for Kobi to say something first. It was a matter of professional respect. Sambinsky was, after all, the detective.

"What do you think will happen when she goes back inside and tells her husband that we were asking about Father Kinga Longokwo? And when she mentions the young victim Kinga?" Oscar understood Kobi's questions were more or less rhetorical.

They walked a few more paces and reached the car. Kobi opened the driver door and paused, looking across the roof at Oscar. He spoke again.

"Why is everyone lying to us?"

TWELVE

Officer Cone looked ready to leap out of her chair.

By the time they'd driven to Tel Aviv Police Headquarters at Salameh 18, she already had a draft report completed. Oscar squirmed as he watched Sambinsky haze her by moving with abnormal deliberateness as he settled into his seat.

In the car, Sambinsky had sat in silence for a few minutes and then clapped the steering wheel with both hands. "Why am I getting the feeling Dumanovsky and Father Longokwo knew each other?" The thought had startled Oscar but somehow hadn't surprised him. Sambinsky had called the office, raising his mobile to his ear while driving – in express contravention of municipal traffic law.

"Cone, I think there a connection between Ruben Dumanovsky and the man called Father Kinga Longokwo. Yes, yes, the priest from Sudan. South Sudan, fine, yes, South Sudan." Oscar could hear a muffled protest emerge from the phone but couldn't make it out. "Okay, okay, you are the one who uncovered Longokwo's visit to Israel. *Kol Hakavod.*" *Well done*, literally *all the respect.* "Can we move on? That's the guy I mean. Can you dig up any connection between these guys? I don't know what it would be. All right, great. I'll see you in half an hour."

Now Officer Cone was sitting opposite Sambinsky tapping a pen on her cheek, waiting for him to give her the go-ahead. They were convened at an ops table in the open plan nerve center of the sprawling police station. Oscar noticed Cone's pen was finer than the usual cop issue ballpoint. Not showy, still mass market, but a gel ink unit of some kind. Something about her discerned the difference acutely enough that she brought her own pen to work. He didn't know what to make of it, but he had come to enjoy the detective's practice of observing details. And this discovery about her, however small, was an interesting enough observation to keep his mind off the deplorable coffee Kobi had handed him. Meanwhile, Sambinsky was doing his best imitation of Victor Borge or the wordless ad executive at the opening of *Planes, Trains, and Automobiles.* He was enjoying torturing his younger cadre too much. Oscar resolved to count backwards from thirty in his mind and then to give Sambinsky a friendly poke.

It wasn't necessary. The detective adjusted his knee against the edge of the table once more and, sipping his coffee, nodded and said, *"Yallah."* Come on.

Angelika Cone burst. "I have not found any direct connection between the two of them yet. *But...* I did find evidence that suggests Ruben Dumanovsky has traveled to Sudan six or seven times in the past twelve years."

Kobi sat up in his chair and put his knee down. "To Sudan?" he asked. "How do you know?"

"I don't know yet, not exactly, but I think so."

Oscar had learned these partial, suggestive proofs were frequent and accepted elements of police investigations in Israel.

It was a derivative of the intelligence culture, which necessarily had to rely on the barest traces of footsteps in the sand. Building a case for prosecution was a different matter. Harder evidence was needed – eventually. But for now, softer echoes would do. Besides, it was her skill at exactly this kind of deduction that had prompted Kobi to recruit her.

"What do you have?" Sambinsky asked.

"The only way – the best way – to get from Tel Aviv to Sudan is through either Istanbul or Addis Ababa." Oscar nodded. He knew most of the routes to and from Africa, and the best were often through Addis. For all he knew, Sambinsky knew them, too. "You can also go through Cairo, but... " She didn't have to finish that sentence, not in Israel. "Dumanovsky has made four trips to Istanbul and three to Addis Ababa in the past twelve years."

"So?"

"And on five occasions, he has returned from Ethiopia. So on at least two of those trips to Istanbul, he wasn't connecting to Mongolia or wherever."

"Good work." Sambinsky pursed his lips. "What else?"

"The most recent trips have been exclusively to and from Addis Ababa. Over the past five years or so, the only way to get to Juba, the new capital of South Sudan, is through Addis Ababa. Istanbul only gets you to Khartoum."

"So as independence comes for South Sudan, and as Juba becomes a feasible destination for airline travel, Dumanovsky starts exclusively going to the only connecting airport that can get him to South Sudan directly from Tel Aviv... "

"*Nachon meod*," she replied. *Exactly right.*

"And who is in South Sudan?" Sambinsky asked. It was a question for the room.

"Father Longokwo or his people... " Oscar supplied the answer.

"Father Longokwo or his people," Inspector Sambinsky repeated, nodding. "So you're going to run down the connecting flights if you can, see if you can put Dumanovsky actually in Sudan?" He looked at Angelika.

"Yes, of course," she said. "It will take some effort to confirm with Sudan and South Sudan immigration. But I can contact Ethiopian Airlines here in Israel and see if I can find a friendly voice. Should I also try to get a hit on his credit cards?"

Sambinsky thought for a moment and said, "No, not now. I don't want to risk his knowing we are digging that deep just yet."

"I also have the CCTV for the street next to the Dolphinarium," Angelika announced.

"Aha! You do!" Sambinsky shouted, raising his arm into the air and attracting the attention of fellow officers walking nearby. They smiled when they saw him. His was a familiar expression of a small victory, well known to the police who shared his workspace. "Some actual, real detective work," he said, beaming at his protégée. "Nicely done, Sherlock." Oscar couldn't help feeling proud of her, too. The sudden change of energy was infectious. "Well, well, show us, show us!" Kobi exclaimed. "What did you see?"

Angelika stood and beckoned them to an audiovisual room. They hovered over the screen as she sat to load it up. She hit play. Grayscale imagery showed exteriors adjacent to the Dolphinarium. The Herbert Samuel road, the next-door park, the pedestrian walkway. This part of Tel Aviv was largely lit by streetlamps and fairly well covered by security cameras. Of course the Dolphinarium itself was not. Inside the gates might as well have been a black hole.

The time stamp on the video showed 4:11 a.m. Even party-on Tel Aviv would be starting to slow its roll. Oscar peered at the screen closely as the action began. A sedan pulled up near the

Dolphinarium. The driver parked between streetlamps, where the shadow of the night was darkest.

"Smart cookies," Sambinsky remarked. Cone nodded.

Four figures stepped out, almost certainly men. They swayed and gesticulated. Even the driver's body language said intoxicated. All wore hats or hoodies, long sleeves, and jeans. The only feature to be seen was a wedge of each of their faces.

Cone pointed. "They've covered up everything. I think it means tattoos."

"Russians, maybe," Sambinsky murmured.

All of them were white, light or dark, perhaps what you might call swarthy, but certainly not black. Then one who had emerged from the back seat turned and reached in. He pulled out another man, skinnier and taller.

And black. African. It was their murder victim. Same clothing. Same figure. He seemed to struggle to stand. The others helped him walk, slinging his arms around their shoulders. The group swayed their way into the Dolphinarium complex. Sambinsky observed a passerby scurrying along the sidewalk without lifting his eyes to the scene of a few Shabbat night drunks heading toward the sea to finish off their evening. Oscar's heart sank. What a lonely moment it must have been for that young man. It might have been his first experience getting drunk. Perhaps his first taste of alcohol. And these evil men had brought him to this place to shoot him in the stomach and head.

At 4:22, no more than eleven minutes after they had arrived, the four men walked back to the car. They were not swaying at all. The purpose of their show of inebriation discharged, it was now time simply to drive away. Their faces were still covered. Oscar drew a breath as he realized how casually they were moving. None of them appeared even moderately anxious. No looking around, no gestures to move faster. Just calm and collected, sauntering away from an act of premeditated murder.

Officer Cone paused the playback and looked at them. She crossed her arms. "No images of their faces. I did get the license plate. It was reported stolen the next day by the owner, a former PR guy for the army, now retired. He lives with his wife and one of their kids now in her early twenties. They're regular citizens. They park it on a tree-lined, dark block."

"Cameras?" Sambinsky asked.

"No cameras. I'm still looking at CCTV from the area the night of the killing. I'm presuming the killers stole it somewhere between 10 p.m. and the time of the murder. The car still hasn't been found. Probably burned somewhere. Maybe we'll get lucky and see a guy getting dropped off on a nearby street to go boost the car."

"Wearing a hoodie," Sambinsky said drily.

"Feels like that, doesn't it?" she replied.

"Yes."

"Feels like what? What does it feel like?" Oscar asked.

"Like they know what they are doing. Like they are not going to get caught on CCTV on the way to steal the car they plan to use to facilitate an assassination."

Silence settled over the small video room as they digested what they'd seen. They were waiting for Sambinsky to speak first.

"Okay. We all know what we need to do," he said.

Angelika nodded and made as if to stand, but Kobi waved at her to stay in her seat. He huddled forward, which had the intended effect of making the others do the same.

"Let's just take stock for a minute and try to understand what the hell is going on. We need to start assembling some picture or another of what happened to the victim and why." He rose, crossed his arms, and sat on the edge of the table. "Victim arrives in town some time in the past one or two weeks... " He trailed off. "Wait, how do we know that?" He looked at Oscar.

"Kuur told us."

"Yes, that's right. And maybe what Kuur says needs to be evaluated with a heavier dose of skepticism than we'd thought." He paused and waved his hand. "Anyway, the guy comes to Israel some time in the past two weeks or something, and Friday night late, early Saturday morning, he is found stumbling with some killers into the Dolphinarium, where they shoot him twice and leave him dead. We find his mouth has a secret cavity in which he stores gold. The gold is confirmed to be of Sudanese origin.

"Into this picture sails Ruben Dumanovsky. The victim had reportedly been seeking a meeting with Dumanovsky. There is circumstantial evidence that the victim succeeded in making contact with him. This evidence includes, so far, CCTV showing the victim in the immediate proximity of Dumanovsky's office and Dumanovsky's reaction when we interviewed him."

"Not to mention the fact that the victim was killed execution style in a well-planned hit by a gang of men who were almost certainly professionals," Cone added, her eyebrows raised to indicate the obviousness of the gangster's connection.

"To be sure, that, too." Sambinsky smiled. "And now we can add to the mix today's revelation from Mrs. Lily Kuur that the mobster Ruben Dumanovsky was hanging around outside the Jebena private club just a few days ago and that somehow, quite coincidentally, the Reverend Pastor Michael—" and he looked at Oscar.

"Michael Alou Kuur Kuur," Oscar supplied.

"The Reverend Pastor Michael Alou Kuur Kuur was savagely beaten by a person or persons he declines to name, perhaps or presumably out of fear rather than out of a sudden fatigue that made him, from one minute to the next, unable to speak to the visitors calling on him at his house."

"Then of course there is the matter of the gold," Oscar ventured.

"Precisely right, Hercule," Sambinsky agreed, his lips pursed approvingly. It was a high form of compliment Sambinsky paid when they found themselves in moments of collaborative detection. Oscar had never had the heart – rather, he had never wanted to do a disservice to his friend's intended generosity with any accidental impoliteness – to explain that Hercule Poirot was, of course, Belgian, and that the memory of Belgians in his home country was, at best, rather mixed. "There is the matter of *ze gold*." Sambinsky affected a terrible French accent. "Our friend Mr. Dumanovsky visits Mr. Kuur, presumably right after learning that the victim was or had been carrying gold on his person around Tel Aviv."

"You told him that?" Officer Cone's mouth gaped.

"Yes. And it was pretty much the only thing we said to him that prompted any kind of reaction," Sambinsky replied.

"I'll say," she retorted. Oscar knew Cone was referring to the theory that Dumanovsky had reacted by beating up Pastor Kuur. He also knew she had intended no insolence toward her boss in saying it. And that her boss would not be offended one way or the other even if she had. *Oh, the Israelis.* If only everyone felt as free to speak their minds so bluntly. He smiled to himself only long enough to remember the damaged condition of Kuur's face, and then he stopped.

"That is exactly right," Sambinsky allowed. "And an unexpected outcome we should all regret. And in any case, we can also wish Mr. Kuur had been a little more forthcoming with us. Now we should be asking ourselves: what does it mean that Dumanovsky, upon learning that this recent arrival from Sudan, whom he may have killed or had killed, was toting an unspecified amount of gold around Tel Aviv, proceeds to deliver such a terrible beating to the Pastor Kuur?" He looked around the table. "Theories? Ideas?"

Ten seconds of silence had to pass before Oscar felt he could conclude that Kobi was actually asking them for theories instead of posing another rhetorical question.

"It means that Ruben Dumanovsky was looking for gold, that Kuur knew that, that Dumanovsky knew that Kuur knew that, and that Dumanovsky believed Kuur must have been holding out on him." Cone looked uncomfortable after blurting it out so energetically. But it was obvious she knew her flow was as logical as a calculator.

"It means that the subject the victim Kinga and the gangster Dumanovsky were discussing, or were meant to discuss, was gold," Oscar said, his voice ending the sentence with an elevated pitch to reflect a level of uncertainty appropriate for the setting. Even though he, like the unsure Angelika, was pretty darn sure.

"*Metzuyan*," Kobi said. *Excellent*. "What else?"

"It probably means," Cone continued, rising, "that Dumanovsky thought either that he had gotten all of the gold he was going to get from the victim or that the victim had none. Which might be the same thing."

"And what do we make of these visits Dumanovsky has been making to Sudan?" The room grew quiet as it became obvious to all of them.

"Dumanovsky is a gold smuggler." Oscar was the first to say it out loud. Sambinsky picked up the thread.

"Twelve years ago, Dumanovsky travels to the country to see what he can find in the chaos. The civil war is tearing the place apart. He has a nose for opportunity, and he quickly learns that the south is hungry for weapons or for cash to buy them. They have gold, precious jewels. They will trade. Dumanovsky is only too happy to oblige."

"Father Longokwo," Oscar said, shaking his head slowly. It was ever the same. *Plus ça change...*

"Somewhere along the line, he meets Father Longokwo."

"I think you have it backwards," Cone interrupted.

"What do you mean?" Oscar asked.

"I mean Longokwo came to Israel before Dumanovsky traveled to Sudan. Longokwo came here in the spring. Dumanovsky went to Sudan for the first time the same year but not until the fall. March vs. October."

"So, what, Father Longokwo comes for Easter, somehow meets Dumanovsky, they make friends, and then Dumanovsky goes to see him in Sudan six months later?" Sambinsky asked.

"Fits, plus or minus?" Cone said it like a question. They knew they were in deep speculative territory, but what else could they do?

"Sounds plausible," Sambinsky nodded. "Let's get sharper on the dates and firm up the travel info, yeah?"

Cone nodded. "Yup, already on it."

"Great. Well, well, well, this gets more and more interesting," Sambinsky said to the ceiling, his eyes closed so he could follow the thread. "Right, where were we? Dumanovsky and Longokwo make a deal. Longokwo gets Dumanovsky gold, diamonds, and whatnot, and Dumanovsky gets Longokwo guns and ammunition for the revolution." He paused and opened his eyes to look at Angelika and Oscar. "Sound right?" he asked. He screwed up his face to show he was not satisfied with the explanation. Oscar twisted his lips rightwards in a demonstration of shared doubt. Angelika squinted and shook her head. "Nah, I agree with you," Sambinsky went on. "Too much. Probably Dumanovsky smuggled the gold and whatever else and paid Father Longokwo or his people in cash."

"Sounds more likely," Cone concurred.

Just then a thought occurred to Oscar. It flew back and forth in his head very fast and landed on his lips. He decided to wait to see if it still seemed true in a minute.

"So one question is how. How did Dumanovsky pay Father Longokwo? How did Longokwo get paid? Did Dumanovsky get cash to Sudan and then organize the smuggling of the gold to Israel? Did the gold come to Israel and then Dumanovsky paid off the courier? Or perhaps the gold and Dumanovsky or his people would bring money to South Sudan after the fact? Something else? All three?"

"What does it matter?" Officer Cone asked.

"It might help us explain what happened to the victim. Did he fail to bring the full shipment of gold? Was he looking for an overdue payment? Was he trying to change the price or the terms of the deal? Or perhaps he was trying to explain that the smuggling would soon cease, now that the war is over, the country of South Sudan is getting on its feet, they have legitimate ways of mining and trading their gold, the South Sudanese authorities are clamping down on unofficial commerce in precious metals and stones, or who knows what else."

"Or perhaps he was the fee," Oscar said slowly. Sambinsky and Cone dropped their heads to listen.

"What?" Sambinsky asked. "You mean like... " He was reluctant to use the word.

"Slavery? You mean slavery?" Angelika filled in the question.

Oscar smiled more broadly than he intended. *White people*, he thought to himself. Sometimes, just sometimes, he wished he wasn't the only African in the room. "No, not slavery. I mean quite the opposite. Smuggling a person to the West. To Israel. To Europe. Even to the United States. In exchange for such and such amount of gold, take this young man and get him safely to a better life where he can get an education, asylum, freedom."

Kobi raised his eyebrows to process the suggestion. Cone

looked at her boss and then at the table and then at her flipbook and then back at her boss.

"Why not?" Sambinsky asked. "It could make sense."

"Because South Sudan is not that bad," Cone said.

"For fuck's sake, we're not here to make political statements about the refugee crisis," Sambinsky said quickly. "Especially not in this unit." He scowled.

"That's not what I meant." She crossed her arms in front of her. "I meant, if you're going to get someone out of South Sudan, you wouldn't have to smuggle them. They could just fly out of Juba and on to wherever they are going and disappear in the cities. Even assuming they can't immigrate officially, there's still no reason he'd schlep overland and through the Sinai in the summer if the main goal was escaping to the West."

"You heard Oscar. The guy was wearing his one set of clothes."

"Still, it's probably not much more expensive to get a ticket to Istanbul and then hitchhike to Greece."

Oscar was impressed with her grit.

"If he had a passport," Kobi said. Then he looked at Oscar to break the tie.

"It is possible," he said diplomatically. The way he said it could have covered nearly everything that anyone had offered all day. Oscar prided himself on soft beginnings. "Probably the very, very poor have far more time than money. For them, overland passage, though slow, is likely cheaper. But Officer Cone's point is well made. Since the relative stability of the independent South Sudan has taken root, it may be less necessary to spirit out a favorite son via illicit means, if finding a better life is the main objective. Which is why I was not referring to the victim of the unfortunate tragedy of the other night. I was referring instead to the man named Kinga of eight years ago."

Cone and Sambinsky nodded and touched their chins to

indicate they would keep listening to his exposition. This was one of Oscar's favorite things about Israel. The old traditions of Talmudic exchange were so much part of the Jewish DNA that even police officers observed them with regularity. When a sage person was expounding, on nearly any subject, it was correct to let him or her continue. On this Kobi clearly agreed. As a young man, he had noticed similar behavior in Japan. It was part of what he had loved about being there.

"At that time," Oscar continued, seeing he had the floor, "smuggling a person would have made much more sense. The war was raging. People were displaced by the tens and hundreds of thousands. South Sudanese were unwanted around the world, and their international status, with or without an accepted passport, was decidedly uncertain. Residents of South Sudan would have had a much more difficult time accumulating currency. Any currency, for that matter. Not to mention banking services that might be needed to establish credit with an airline or travel agency. Never mind electronic payments." He paused and looked for questions.

"You said 'favorite son,'" Mefake'ah Sambinsky asked.

"I did. I suspect the earlier Kinga of eight years ago was a relative of the erstwhile priest Father Longokwo. Perhaps even his son. If I had to guess, I would probably say he was his son. The name, the specific exclusion of tribal scarring on his visible body parts, even the fact of his arrival, all point to his being a personage of some distinction in the Toposa community. Now that we know – now that we suspect – Mr. Ruben Dumanovsky had some ongoing commerce with Father Longokwo, it is not too far fetched to surmise that part of the deal at some point included bringing Longokwo's son or nephew to Israel."

"Bravo, Oscar. It seems to fit," Sambinsky said.

"Thank you. I agree it is the only explanation that seems to answer all of the facts we have gathered to date. Now the question remains: why did the young Kinga come to Israel in the first place? Perhaps he came to verify some business dealings. Perhaps he was here only briefly before returning to the country of his birth." He waited for someone to state the obvious. It didn't take long.

"No way," Sambinsky replied.

"I agree it seems unlikely. Why would he return to South Sudan in the bloodiest depth of its conflict, when so much of the population was seeking to flee? By contrast, it seems more likely that his transfer to Israel was an element of the transaction. Payment in kind, let us say, for gold and diamonds smuggled out of Sudan and into Israel."

"Isn't it just speculation?" Cone seemed a little annoyed.

"Yes. It is. Perhaps we will never know what happened. But right now I can't think of a better outline. Can you?" Sambinsky asked. His tone was gentle. He was actually asking her opinion, not insinuating she should shut up. That happened other times and sounded different.

"No, I can't," Cone said, drumming her fingers. "But who the hell knows."

"Someone knows," Sambinsky pronounced.

"Forgive me," said Oscar. "But perhaps I may continue. I agree it is speculative, but maybe you will find it illuminating nonetheless. Not long after the Kinga of eight years ago arrives here, he disappears. According to our friend Pastor Michael Kuur, the earlier Kinga is around for only a month or two, which is not much longer than the time we believe Father Longokwo spent here four years earlier. In any event, one or two months hardly sounds like a leisure tour of this beautiful country." He smiled at his own humor. Then he steepled his hands in the manner of classic detectives he had read about in early crime novels. Then just as fast, he put his hands down, feeling ridiculous. "So the question is begged: what happened to him?

Did he travel on to Europe or the States? Or did he meet with a worse fate? And if he did, why?" He stood up and placed his hands in his pockets. "Now we advance even further toward the edge of speculation. Is there any clue we might glean from the events of this Shabbat that might shed light on what happened to the earlier Kinga from eight years ago?" He leaned against the wall. "This has been turning in my mind since we first learned about the mysterious prior Kinga. But when we discovered that Father Longokwo himself had visited Eretz Israel, and when we subsequently understood Dumanovsky and Father Longokwo were likely business partners, something seemed to fall into place. You see, Father Longokwo died in South Sudan not so long after the prior Kinga arrived in Israel and disappeared. I believe some time in the following year or perhaps two. If harm did befall the young man, there was probably not enough time for Father Longokwo to make proper inquiries or even retaliate before he died. Suppose Father Longokwo were asking about the young Kinga's radio silence after his short sojourn in Israel. A practiced liar like Dumanovsky may have been able to string him along with various furnished reasons for months and months. Perhaps Father Longokwo grew suspicious. But in any case, he died. Now that we are saying it, one wonders whether Father Longokwo died under suspicious circumstances. Perhaps Dumanovsky tired of Father Longokwo's persistence and authored his death? Who knows. All of the conventional wisdom is that he died a beloved hero of his people at an old age. No matter, for the moment. There is still a question that has lain around for nearly a decade. What happened to the young man Kinga? Why has no one heard from him?"

Oscar crossed the small room and leaned against the AV console.

"Now we come to the present day. A young man, perhaps eighteen years old, perhaps a touch younger or older, bearing the same tribal markings and calling himself by the same name, makes his way to Israel. He is quite an unusual young man. For example, he demonstrates at least two acts of great courage or conviction. First, he crosses overland into this country at what must have been great personal peril. Greater still, given the regional conditions, than the earlier Kinga would have faced. Second, he subjected himself to a dental procedure of considerable pain. The removal of a molar tooth probably without the benefits of contemporary anesthetic would have caused him unimaginable suffering. Yet he did it. So... " He squared his shoulders, stood away from the wall, and asked the others: "Who was he, and why did he come here?"

They were silent.

"*Nu?*" Sambinsky said. *So? Well?*

"I believe he was the younger brother of the first Kinga. Perhaps a cousin. But if I had to guess, he was his brother. Only a child when his brother departed Sudan, arrived in Israel, and then disappeared. He was unable to do anything then. Then their father died. Having come of age, and having never forgotten the question, he came to get answers. He came to confront Dumanovsky."

Sambinsky was about to say *metzuyan – excellent*, when Cone interjected. "Or did he come to carry on the business arrangement with Dumanovsky?"

"That could well be," Oscar nodded. "They are not mutually exclusive concepts. However, I imagine that, if anything, the new Kinga may have been seeking to reestablish such a business arrangement. Or to collect on some long-overdue obligation. Assuming that he was not totally distracted by the memory of a missing brother and that he wanted to do any commerce with Dumanovsky at all, I believe those explanations are more likely. In other words, I would hazard that any standing arrangement between Dumanovsky and Father Longokwo expired soon after the erstwhile priest's death and that Dumanovsky has carried on his South Sudanese affairs with other contacts since then."

"It makes more sense if the new Kinga is here in Israel to settle a score," Sambinsky said, notching his thumb in his belt to help him think. "A personal one or a business matter or both. He comes to Israel, confronts Dumanovsky, and that gets him killed. Certainly, it is clarifying as a theory. Keeps it all in one picture."

"Is it useful?" Cone asked the sensible question.

Sambinsky raised his palms upward and bobbed his head side to side. "Yeah. Why not? At least it gives us a line of inquiry on Ruben Dumanovsky." He looked at Oscar. "That was a tour de force, Hercule."

Oscar beamed a smile back to telegraph he was hardly offended by the assessment that his conjecture may not have been adjudged wholly useful. He agreed.

"Another piece of the puzzle may be said to be falling elegantly into place," he said, feeling heady. "The timeline Officer Cone has been assembling for Mr. Dumanovsky matches the rise in his fortunes. He seems to have become quite wealthy at around the same moment he made contacts with the South Sudanese."

"I didn't know you read the society pages, Oscar," Kobi said. "Follow the celebrities and gangsters, do you?"

"More like social media." Cone sought to join the joke.

"Or perhaps such information is to be found in the pages of *Haaretz*," Oscar grinned.

Sambinsky rapped the table. "Okay, kids, enough kibitzing for one day. Officer Cone, you know what to do. Keep going on Dumanovsky's travel details. We have to go brace Michael Kuur again, but not today. He's too fragile, and we don't have anything new to ask him yet."

"One more thing." Cone wasn't done. She was already assimilating her boss's Columbo habit. "Why, if Father

Longokwo could travel commercial, couldn't his son Kinga do the same? I mean the Kinga son from eight years ago."

Oscar nodded. "Yes, but please recall that by then the war had engulfed South Sudan. There would have been no way to depart without special transport. Access to the Khartoum airport would have been impossible without specific permission, and, since Father Longokwo would have been a top enemy of Sudan by then, his kin would never have been granted access. Juba's airport was barely functional for anything resembling commercial aircraft then. No. His son would have been better off overland."

THIRTEEN

I t was not quite 4:30 by the time Oscar sat at a sidewalk table at La Mer beach bar. On days when he wore his work shoes, which was most days, and especially on days when he wore his dress slacks, socks, and shirt for a meeting with his immigration advocate, he would not sit at the tables in the sand but instead up on the concrete.

The view was the same. The only real difference was you could not feel the beach in your toes, which was, at those times, exactly right. Four p.m. was one of his most perfect hours for coming here. In sixty or seventy minutes, the beach and the bar would be teeming with people. But if you could somehow manage to get there sooner, the Mediterranean was yours. You could choose any chair and stay for as long as you wanted, feeling the breeze pick up as you sipped a beer or coffee or smoked hookah if you preferred.

The Americano was on Oscar's table almost as soon as he had seated himself. He never ordered anything else. He looked at the sea, smiled, felt the sun on his face, and marveled at how unlikely his existence – this existence – was. He nearly felt moved to say another Shehecheyanu, but he decided against it, lest he accidentally debase the prayer from overuse. The Shehecheyanu was such a superb blessing. And as a convert to Judaism, he felt a special duty to treat the *brachot* gingerly.

Oscar released one button at the top of his shirt and rolled his sleeves. As he approached forty years of age – he chose not to dwell on how closely he was approaching it – he was becoming more aware of himself. He was learning, for example, just how much he was a man of ritual. If pressed, he could probably count dozens of rituals in his everyday life. Roll up the sleeves to mark the end of the day. Unbutton the top one to mark a moment of relaxation. Observe a ban on screens at breakfast in his flat. Pour himself Havana Club like a waiter before sitting at the table to sip it. Polish his shoes on Thursday evening whether they needed it or not. Crisp the linens before reading on top of the duvet. Never under it. Crisp them again before turning down the corner like a maid and getting in. Americanos for the morning. Americanos for the day. Americanos for night. Set out the tin of Ashton Esquires and the glass ashtray on the windowsill even if he was not going to smoke. Oscar had spent more than enough time with victims of sustained trauma to know very well that the creation of heavy ritual was a common coping mechanism for people whose lives had been upturned. No matter how much or how often he wanted to distinguish himself from the refugees he helped on a daily basis – his education, his outlook, his... everything, he felt – he had to admit sometimes that he was, after all, just like them: a man who had suffered terrible displacement. Of course, some of it must be attributable to his living in such a tiny space. How else to create separation of activities, of work and leisure, within it? And yet, he grinned whenever he thought about it, there may also be something to be said for his being, well, perhaps a little obsessive–compulsive. He didn't feel it did him any harm. A touch of OCD suited a polite person. In many circumstances, light OCD could be difficult to distinguish from politeness. And then there was the possibility that he was built for ritual. In his youth, he would wake earlier than his family to seize some alone time in the kitchen of their house or sit outside before the sunrise. He had long enjoyed marking time. In Oscar's observation, a principal cause of the basic emotive suffering of the modern people around him was that they didn't. People who marked time were generally happier. He certainly liked it, anyway.

Perhaps that was one of the reasons he had been drawn so quickly to Judaism. There was a prayer to mark everything.

The Americano was good. It was always good, but sometimes, like now, it was better. No doubt Ori was in the house. He was one of the owners, and he invariably manned the coffee machine when he was around. He was one of those Israeli men who kept lean and fit well into his sixties. His private hobby was building a recreational vehicle from scratch. He showed Oscar photos of the progress from time to time. It looked like a semi with an extended cab painted race car red. It even had a yellow flame on the door. Ori's plan was to retire, transport the vehicle to Greece by boat, and spend the rest of his life driving around the world in it. Of course, he joked, there was no way to take a road trip from Israel that didn't start by boat. Unless you were in a tank. Ori had married a rich woman in Moscow and saw her somewhere in the world once per month. He felt his life was wonderful. Oscar liked him. Talking with Ori made him feel older and younger at the same time.

Oscar thought of Lily. As his mind turned to his age, he would often wonder if he would ever marry. He had never gotten close. There wasn't much history to speak of. There was Lucille, his girlfriend from university. He had loved her. He was almost certainly going to marry her, up until the time he had fled Kinshasa. They had stayed in touch for some time, and Oscar had imagined he would return and be reunited with her. But after a while, they spoke less regularly, and she found someone else.

Then in Israel he had met Gili. They had both been young and adrift for one reason or another, he because of his itinerancy, she because of a complicated family history. It hadn't worked. The drugs she used were light but too much for him to be around. Then there were a couple of attractions that he knew boiled down in no small part, as far as the ladies were concerned, to a mixture of his exoticness and the hangdog flavor of his story. He had become fed up with that silliness. For a long time – for a number of years he preferred not to remember precisely – there had been a drought befitting the Dead Sea. But he did miss being with a woman. All of it. Most of it, anyway. Their hips included, especially in this country. And he shared the dream of most men and women of one day having a family. G–d will provide, he usually thought. And then he understood also it might behoove him to take some more active part in G–d's plan.

Ah, that woman Lily, he chuckled. *What a jewel.* He chastised himself for being so immediately and ridiculously smitten. But that was the nature of nature, was it not? He chastised himself even more for thinking of his friend's wife in this way. Even if that, too, was the nature of nature, the oldest laws there were forbade it. But nevertheless: if he just let the thought of her inspire him to look for another woman, perhaps there was not much grievous harm in that.

Why, Michael Kuur, you lucky fellow! Even older than I, Oscar thought to himself, and together with such a young and beautiful girl. He raised his Americano to the horizon, nodded his head, and sipped. He clasped his hands together across his belly. This girl Lily must have struck Pastor Kuur in much the same way she'd struck him. He had never seen the pastor with a woman before. Never heard him whisper about one. Maybe he had even sent for Lily from Sudan. Perhaps that was how he had met her. *Sly devil.* To have a girl like that. Imagine what it would be like to talk to her, all afternoon and into the night. To have the privilege of gazing at her without having to look away. *Well, there was the one time,* Oscar recalled. Michael had confided in Oscar once. It was late, in the Jebena, perhaps four years ago. They had been having a good time, drinking guhwah and talking about their fathers. Each competed to be the son of the more domineering and eccentric man. Oscar had recounted a favorite tale of his upbringing, in which his father, having been disappointed by his low marks on a mathematics examination, required him to solve a formula before taking each and every single bite of his supper. Michael had told a story in which his father, having learned from his teacher that he had misbehaved at school, marched him to his teacher's house at dinner time and forced him to apologize and then to clean the kitchen and the outdoor latrine while he waited with his arms crossed over a long switch. Oscar laughed again now as he recalled it. Kuur was a terrific raconteur. As the hour grew late, Kuur had gone to the back of his club and retrieved a bottle of whiskey and two elegant glasses. Oscar had rarely drunk scotch before or since, but they polished off a few fingers that night. As he'd reached the start of his fourth pour, Kuur's smile had changed into a forlorn moue and then into a wistful frown.

"You know, Oscar, I was in love once."

Oscar could still remember the sharpness of his sense that the mood had changed instantly, that something was about to be said that was so intimate it might be sacred. He had never heard Kuur utter anything that was actually revealing. That much was not unusual: most men he knew were like that.

As soon as Kuur spoke, Oscar felt privileged and elated. Without a doubt the alcohol amplified his feeling. Kuur was still. He hung his head over his knees. Then he took a sip directly from the bottle. Oscar couldn't help feeling surprised. It was his club, after all, and his whiskey, so he could do what he liked. Kuur was amongst friends. But it was so unlike him. And the scotch must have been so expensive. The drink was darker and smokier than anything else he'd tasted in his life. Oscar could recall that the name began with a La, like Lam- or Lap- or Lag- or something else, but he had never seen a bottle like it since.

The tension in the large, empty room was sensational. It went on for second after second, this silence, then a full minute and what must have been another and then a third. Still Kuur said nothing.

Eventually Oscar couldn't stand it. He clapped Kuur's back. "Michael, do tell, you're with a friend. It's just you and me here. Tell me all about her, please!" He had of course intended it as a warm invitation to share intimacy. But he had gravely misread the coffee grounds. Some men just need a long silence to build their courage before they can reveal themselves. Oscar had interrupted Kuur's. Michael turned his head, smiled at Oscar, and tapped him on the knee as if to say, it's okay. But Oscar could see a tear welling up in his eye. He felt horrified, like the murderer of a precious, quiet flicker that might have given life to a deeper friendship had it not been snuffed out by his hand. Kuur stood and made as if to get ready to lock up.

That was the time when Oscar Orleans learned the importance of waiting in stillness for the other person to say his or her piece.

He had never come to hear the story of Kuur's former flame. But he was glad for the pastor that the chance had come back around. *Good work, Michael. To second loves for older young men.* Oscar smiled at his own humor.

The mobile phone buzzed in his pocket. Oscar thought he must remember to add to his end of day demarcation the ritual shutting off of his phone. Or at least of the alerts. Or at the very least of the buzzing. He fished it out with two fingers and looked. It was a WhatsApp from Kobi. If there was one technology that could be uninvented, he thought to himself.

"Can I send you a video?" Kobi wanted to know.

"No Wi-Fi here. Is it urgent?" he replied.

"You're going to want to see this. New CCTV. Come in the morning."

FOURTEEN

Oscar crossed the threshold of Police Headquarters just after 8 a.m. Sambinsky would have been there for one hour already, and he could only guess when Cone had arrived, if she had gone home at all. For the police, when it was on, it was on. Oscar had been up early, too, but he had understood from Kobi's invitation that he needn't rush, so he walked to Shuk Ha'Carmel for a civilized macchiato and a labaneh. He dipped the bread into the yogurt and ate slowly. After years of visiting the same stands at the open air market, the food remained inexplicably delicious. The Israelis, he thought. Half their best delicacies are Arabic, and another quarter are Persian or Turkish. And one hundred percent of the neighbors spent eighty percent of their leisure time communicating on Israeli-made devices and social media. When would these poor children figure it out? He sighed and thought of Africa. Admittedly, he considered, even worse.

"Sherlock Cones found something very interesting." Kobi waved and greeted him. Sambinsky's voice was loud enough for the other officers on the floor to hear. It was his way of paying her psychic compensation. Oscar caught her lowering her head but beaming with pride. "Let's go into the AV room. Angelika, tee it up."

"Look here," she said, pointing at the screen. "You recognize it?"

"It's Hatachana Merkazit, the main bus station," Oscar replied.

"*Nachon meod.*" *Exactly.* "Four days before the victim died. Now look here. Look carefully." She touched the image to focus his attention. "Recognize him?"

A tall, skinny African walked from the bus platform across the screen and toward the terminal building. He was wearing a large camping backpack over both shoulders. A bedroll was strapped to the top of the bag.

"Is that Kinga?" Oscar asked.

"Wait a second. Let me do a close-up." Cone zoomed in on the man's face. "And now another angle... " She switched to a different camera. She moved the film back and forth. The pictures were all grayscale, grainy from close-up, and a little blurry from the motion. But the South Sudan jersey was the same. The features, too. The young man was clearly Kinga.

"What is he doing with a rucksack?" Oscar said.

"I'm wondering the same thing," Kobi agreed. "And look at it. That's not a school book bag. That's a huge backpack for some overnight camping. Now check out what Cone noticed yesterday evening. She's been reviewing the video like a madwoman."

"Look at his shirt." She paused the video and pointed. "Now look at his pants. And now... look especially at his sandals."

"He is covered in dust," Oscar remarked. "But why? He must have created a mess on the bus."

"And thank G–d for that," Sambinsky said. "While you were taking your beauty rest, Officer Cone was doing some real detective work. She went to the station, showed the picture to some drivers, and one guy recognized him. He said he had picked up the victim at Ein Bokek."

"At the Dead Sea?" Oscar exclaimed.

"Yes. The driver said he remembered him well because he was African, but also because he was so dusty. Very dusty. Left a trail in the bus and on the seats."

"Was he on holiday?" Oscar asked, incredulous.

"Actually, what the driver said was interesting," she continued. "He said he was accustomed to passengers who have traces of Dead Sea mud on their bodies. But that mud is dark. And it cakes. The victim was dusty – the driver kept saying dusty – and the dust on him was much lighter, like a yellow or red."

"I have no idea. What was he doing out there?"

"Camping?" Sambinsky asked.

"Who the hell goes camping at the Dead Sea? I have never heard of it."

"Some people do," Sambinsky offered. But it was clear he didn't think it made sense, either.

"Believe me," Oscar said, "there is about zero point zero chance that this boy – that this Toposa, who has probably spent ninety percent of his nights on earth staring at a starry sky – scrambled his way overland from the southeastern districts of South Sudan to Eretz Israel so that he might take a bus to the Dead Sea for some recreational camping!" He startled himself with his vigor. The room paused. Then Kobi nodded his head and twisted his chin.

"No shit," he said. "But we can't figure out what the deal was. We thought you might have a notion."

"There's something else," Cone spoke up. Sambinsky raised his eyebrows. Apparently he hadn't heard the latest. "I've spent almost eight hours looking at every video I could get from the Hatachana CCTV from the days before to see if I could find out when the victim had traveled out to Ein Bokek. There's only one bus per day. So I started there. Then I branched out to the times when buses leave for Jerusalem, thinking maybe he made a connection to a bus from there to the Dead Sea. The buses for Jerusalem run pretty much all day, so I had to cover most of the time every single day. That didn't work. So I went back a few more days. Nothing. Then a few more days. Still nothing."

"So? *Nu?* What did you find?" Sambinsky was eager.

"So far nothing. Maybe I missed him, I haven't slept much. I'll look again. But I'm already back into the week before last. So either I missed him or he took some other means of transport to get to the Dead Sea in the first place, or—"

"Or he was out there for a lot longer than we would have guessed."

"And he was in the country for more than the week or two Kuur told us he was here," said Oscar.

Sambinsky growled. "First he lies to us about never having met him. Lily says the victim was in their damn flat. Now we know he's probably lying to us about how long he was in the country. Can someone give me one good reason I shouldn't go arrest that son of a bitch for murder right now?"

Cone and Oliver looked at each other. There was no real arguing with it. But of course there were reasons. Kobi knew them, too, and he was going to say them in a minute.

"Ruben Dumanovsky," Kobi offered at last, exhaling. "He's involved somehow. And I doubt Kuur killed anyone. He certainly didn't send a four-man white-guy hit squad to bring the victim to the Dolphinarium and shoot him in the head."

Oscar nodded. Too soon, apparently. Kobi flared again.

"But I'll tell you what: that motherfucker better not lie to us again, Oscar. You tell him. You go see him and tell him."

FIFTEEN

"You ready for more bullshit?" Sambinsky asked as they trudged up the stairs.

It was after eleven by the time they approached Dumanovsky's Pasternak Design Build Develop office on Allenby Street. After their morning conference, Kobi had left Cone to it and taken Oscar for shakshuka at a particular shakshuka shithole Oscar detested. Everything about the enterprise enervated him. He was not hungry. He did not want to watch Kobi eat. He did not want to eat shakshuka. He did not want to eat at this crappy shakshuka place.

Shakshuka was the rare delicacy of Israeli cuisine Oscar did not understand. *Delicacy*. That was overstating it. The dish was eggs and tomatoes. Some people added onions. Big deal. It was boring. Worse still, Israel worshipped shakshuka. Everyone's mom made the best. Everyone's bubbe made it better. The food was a national madness.

Of course he could never say anything out loud. He would never. To be a guest in this country, to be an aspiring Israeli, one had to keep mum about certain subjects. Not the occupation.

Not the territories. Not an undivided Jerusalem. Not Labor or Likud or Netanyahu or the other one. You could say what you wanted about those. But shut up about shakshuka. They'd look at you like an alien. Which he was already.

Oscar watched Kobi slurp up the hot skillet with a tablespoon. He made a show of having a few bites. Kobi finished and stretched back to ease the pressure over his belt. He noticed Oscar wasn't eating, so he gestured and Oscar nodded, and Kobi switched plates and continued.

It was all so backwards, Oscar thought. From time to time, after he'd given a lecture to a tour group of Jews from New York or Los Angeles, they would invite him to *fress* – to eat gustily – the pastrami and corned beef they had brought with them from the States. *That* was food. Why could the nation state of the Jews not trade shakshuka for deli meats and creamed herring? Even in the context of the topsy turvy world that was Israel, this was standout backwards. You couldn't find pastrami anywhere in the country like the stuff they brought from America.

Now it was time to see Dumanovsky again. The late morning sun was strong, and the windowed stairwell had already grown stuffy with heat.

"Yes, I am ready," Oscar answered as they reached the landing.

Kobi knocked. The same squat woman opened the door. She offered no expression of recognition. Oscar wondered if having an amnesiac receptionist might be useful in the mob business.

"I am Mefake'ah Sambinsky of the Israel Police, Tel Aviv District. Is Mr. Dumanovsky in?"

A blast of cold air emerged from the door. The Pasternak team must have had their thermostat all the way down.

"I know who you are," she responded, sounding very much like someone who was not an amnesiac. She managed to speak almost entirely without moving a single part of her face. "Please wait here." She closed the door. For some reason Oscar could not tell, Kobi did not protest. They could hear footsteps, some murmuring, and more footsteps. She opened the door again and made room for them to enter.

There was more bustle in the office than there had been the last time. Three people milled about a table in the room to the left. One was a young man, svelte and manicured, in a suit and tie that would not have looked out of place in a men's magazine. He had light skin and a clean-shaven face and one of those ski jump haircuts that Oscar thought looked stupid. Another was a burly fellow, maybe forties, maybe middle thirties, it was hard to tell with Russians, if they were Russians, they aged so terribly. He was wearing a collared shirt and a light sweater, which would have been unnecessary but for the air conditioning. He was peering over or through reading glasses at documents on the table, marking them with a pen. He glanced up at the visitors and back down. Careless thick stubble covered his face. The third was a short, stunning, fair-skinned blonde. She wore a dark suit to match the younger man's, bright red heels and lipstick in what appeared to be the exact same hue. A sheer buttoned blouse was open far enough to reveal cleavage. Both Kobi and Oscar compelled themselves to steer their eyes away from her so as not to be distracted and to steer their eyes away from each other so as not to let slip an unprofessional reaction. The woman looked at them briefly. Or, rather, she looked through them, practiced as she must have been at taking in oglers in the middle distance corner of a thousand-meter stare.

Dumanovsky opened the door to his private office on the right. He walked back in as if to imply the visitors should follow him. Sambinsky led. As they entered his office, he was seating himself in a black leather and steel chair behind a glass desk and indicating for them to sit opposite. Still he said nothing. Even after they were seated, he remained silent, his hands clasped casually in front of him on the desk. To Oscar's eye, this guy looked so relaxed he might as well have been dead.

"Mr. Dumanovsky, I can remind you that I am Mefake'ah Sambinsky of the Israel Police, Tel Aviv District. You are not obligated to speak to me. I would like to ask if you know a Michael Alou Kuur Kuur. He is often known as Pastor Kuur or Michael Kuur. Do you know this person?"

Dumanovsky was too smart to say no. Kobi knew. Dumanovsky knew he knew. So there was only one answer.

"Yes."

"What is the nature of your relationship?"

"I have met him." His hands and body didn't move. His mouth did. He barely blinked. He could have been a lizard. Oscar tried to remain equally still but felt a small itch disturb his neck.

"When did you last see him?"

"Recently."

"When?"

"I'm not sure."

"Why did you go see him?"

"I didn't say I went to see him."

"He came to see you?"

"From time to time I am able to arrange for some in the refugee community to get work in construction. Jobs."

"You hire refugees to do construction work?"

"Mefake'ah Sambinsky wishes to visit me to discuss labor policy? If I am suspected of violating employment laws, I will call my lawyer. It is possible to cease giving refugees work." He gazed directly at Oscar, as if he knew exactly how the police department must have been paying this particular African refugee. Kobi waited for the moment of sly indignation to pass. Dumanovsky looked at him and spoke again. "In this nation of immigrants, I wish more people would give refugees opportunity."

"Did you visit Pastor Michael Kuur last week?"

"Probably."

"What did you talk about?" Sambinsky opened a notebook to telegraph an increased level of seriousness. Even this was scary enough to make some interviewees sweat. Not this one. Dumanovsky paused and turned his head to look outside. From his chair he could see the sidewalk on the other side of the street. A popular coffee place was in full pre-lunch throng.

"Is there something I can help you with?" he asked, affecting boredom in a way Oscar thought was just a little too forceful.

"Mr. Dumanovsky," Kobi crossed his legs at the knee, "is there a particular reason you have visited Sudan so many times?"

The Russian's face gave a tremor. It was fast, fleeting, but Oscar caught it. He was sure Kobi would have caught it, too. Now they knew Dumanovsky had, in fact, traveled to Sudan. Angelika would confirm it, but she didn't need to. His reaction had just done it for her.

"It is a beautiful country," Dumanovsky said. His left eyebrow rose and fell again. Perhaps it was his way of expressing casualness. Perhaps it was an attempt to work the furrowing of his forehead as he endeavored to estimate how much the police knew. "And it is new country, like Israel," he added with a measure of passion, "hopeful place, like Israel."

"You mean South Sudan," Kobi said warmly, and Dumanovsky's expression fell as he realized he had made his first mistake. Emphasizing the newness of the place confirmed he had been in the south.

"Yes." He managed a smile. "I like South, and I like North also."

"Is it difficult for Israelis in the North?" Sambinsky cocked his head.

"How do you mean? Because of Muslims? Bah! People don't care there. They have other problems. Sometimes, sure, but mostly not." He leaned back in his chair and looked past their heads at the paintings on the wall behind them. Oscar had noticed them when he came in. They were Andy Warhol type knockoffs, bright colors and simple themes. "I have been going to Sudan for more than ten years. Probably you know this." He picked up a pen and twirled it. "Big construction boom. There was big boom. Many Israelis have been in Africa on big projects. Civil engineers. Civil projects. Then of course there was crash during war. Very sad. But still some projects to work on, finish. Then after situation stable, more projects come back."

"That's all you do there, Ruben?" Kobi asked. Using his first name had the desired effect of antagonizing him. Dumanovsky looked at him hard, controlling his sense of insult. "Just construction?"

"Construction, projects, building, architecture, design, develop, civil engineer."

"No smuggling, Ruben?" Sambinsky smiled knowingly. There was a pause. Oscar felt uncomfortable in the midst of the violent tension that hung in the chilled air between them. Dumanovsky could have leapt directly from his chair, across the desk, and stabbed Kobi in the neck with his pen before Oscar could do anything about it.

"Hahahahaha!" Dumanovsky suddenly threw back his head and broadcast a loud, knee-slapping guffaw. "Very good, Inspector! You very funny guy!"

"Yes, thank you, Ruben, it is funny, isn't it?" Sambinsky replied, continuing to smile knowingly. "Well, thank you, we will be in touch." He rose quickly and left before Dumanovsky could walk him out. Oscar followed, surprised at the speed and that Kobi did not pause to do a Columbo. Less than two minutes later, they were on the street.

"He is neck deep in that country," Sambinsky said as they walked down the block toward his car. Oscar agreed. He tried to make some sense of the arc of Dumanovsky's time in Sudan, but he could not come up with anything off the top of his head.

Kobi stopped on the sidewalk and looked up at Oscar, his hand covering his eyes from the glare of the sun. "What if he went to Sudan the first time as a businessman. He is hustling for his company like any other guy. Somewhere along the line he comes across Longokwo or maybe even someone else. The war breaks out. His valuable contracts evaporate. At the same time, the warring factions are cash starved and need weapons. He finds a new line of work."

"It sounds very plausible, Inspector," Oscar answered.

"Yes, but does it get us any closer to proving Dumanovsky killed that kid?"

SIXTEEN

Sambinsky raced down Allenby, pulled left on Jaffa and a hard right on to HaGalil Street. Oscar clasped his armrest as Kobi dodged sedans and trucks and peeled past a gaggle of girls on foot. As they approached the block where Kuur lived, Sambinsky slowed suddenly and pulled into a spot that edged halfway onto the sidewalk.

"Look, look!" He pointed, ducking his body low in his seat. Oscar reflexively did the same and peered across the dash. There was Lily Kuur, holding her baby Nellie, strolling in the other direction.

"Out for a walk?" Oscar observed.

"*Nachon meod.*" *Exactly right.* "We can talk with him alone. Come on."

They stepped out of the car and were up the stairs in less than a minute. Kobi knocked. He knocked again, louder.

The door swung slowly open. Kuur squinted his eyes from pain and the sun. He had probably not been outside since his injury. Through all the bandages he looked taken aback, maybe frightened. He sighed. Kobi stretched out his hand forcefully to hold the door open. There was little chance Kuur would have tried to close it, but Sambinsky was sending a message.

"You lied, Kuur." Sambinsky's tone was matter of fact. "You said you never met the victim. Your wife told us he was here in your house. You told me he had been in Israel for only one or two weeks. We know for a fact he was here longer than that." He softened his voice to a soothing tone. "I understand you are afraid to tell us what you know. But it is the only way I can be of any help to you at all. Otherwise, you are the main suspect in a murder case."

Kuur looked defeated. His lean against the hallway wall shifted into a slump, and his eyes filled with tears. He drew himself together and shuffled down the hall. Kobi and Oscar followed. Kobi helped him ease into the same chair by the window and then joined Oscar on the couch.

"I *am* afraid," Kuur said.

"Of whom?" Sambinsky asked gently.

Kuur paused. The grief covered his face like a mask.

"Pastor, I cannot help you unless you tell me," Kobi continued. When he wanted to be, he could be gentle. It was disarming. "Of Dumanovsky? Of Ruben Dumanovsky?"

Kuur nodded. Even that small acknowledgment was enough to release him from a huge burden. He began sobbing. His shoulders shook up and down, and he brought his right hand to his heart to touch his chest, which heaved with his tears. "Oh G–d. Dear G–d," he lowed, then again, "Oh G–d. Dear G–d."

Oscar felt his anguish. He knew they just had to wait it out. But he had seen this torment before, a combination of terror from a horrible, powerful menace and suffering from a baneful loss. They were usually amplified by obligatory silence. The release was always an emotional flood. Oscar had seen it many times, too many to count, over the years, first in Africa, in Congo, in

Kinshasa, then on the journey north, and in Israel, after the suicide attacks.

Kobi rose and returned from the kitchen with a glass of cold water. Kuur grasped it with both hands and drank it down in one go. He wiped the tears from his eyes. That this man of impeccable manners did not seek to apologize was evidence enough of his pain.

"Did Dumanovsky do this to you?" Kobi asked.

Kuur nodded again.

"What happened?"

Kuur only shook his head slowly.

"Tell me what happened, Michael." Kobi reached for Lily's chair, pulled it close to Kuur and sat. "I can put that piece of shit away. Tell me. I will make an arrest, and you'll never have to worry about him again."

"Lily... Nellie... " Kuur whispered.

"He won't be able to hurt any of you," Kobi said. "Help me help you. Please, Michael. You can trust me." Kobi glanced at Oscar for affirmation. Oscar looked at Kuur, but the pastor's eyes were affixed to the floor.

"I think he is responsible for what happened to that young man," he said, his voice quiet but clear.

"Why? What do you know?" Kobi asked. Kuur said nothing.

"Which young man do you mean, Pastor?" Oscar leaned forward from the couch.

"The young man who disappeared," Kuur said, looking over to Oscar. "He was a wonderful boy." There was a short silence as the detective digested the information.

"How do you know? What happened?"

Kuur eased his head back into the blanket covering his chair and closed his eyes. He looked exhausted. Kobi pressed the case. "Pastor." He tapped his hand. "Michael, you must tell us what you know." Kuur opened his eyes. They were filled with fatigue and fear.

"Michael, what about the victim from Shabbat? What about him? What do you know about what happened to him? Did Dumanovsky have him killed? Did he kill the second Kinga?"

Kobi looked at Oscar, who stared back helplessly. Oscar could tell they both felt like idiots.

"Michael!" Kobi raised his voice a decibel, perhaps to keep him awake or perhaps out of frustration. "Talk to me! Why did the young man go to the Dead Sea? Do you know why the victim was at the Dead Sea last week? What was he doing there, Michael? What is at the Dead Sea?" He was nearly shouting now, and the more he did, the more Kuur looked like he'd had a stroke. He was withdrawing completely. "Dammit, Michael. Wake up and give me something. Why did the Shabbat victim go to the Dead Sea?"

Footsteps approached from the entrance hallway. Kobi went quiet. Oscar turned around. Kuur's eyes closed as his breathing slowed.

Lily appeared from around the corner, her baby nestled against her hip and looking alert and curious. Her eyes were large and round, like her mother's. Lily was clearly startled. Oscar felt his mouth go dry as he took her in. Even flustered and sweaty from a tour around the neighborhood on a hot day with her baby in tow, she looked like fresh air. Her neck slid elegantly into a dark red summer frock.

"Inspector, Mr. Orleans," she bowed. "What a surprise. We did not expect you." She placed the baby on the couch next to Oscar, flattened her dress with her hands, and crossed to her husband's chair. She touched his forehead, examined his bandages, and adjusted the blanket behind his head. Kuur's breathing was heavy now, as if he might actually be asleep. She turned and looked Sambinsky in the eyes.

"Inspector, I am afraid my husband is not well. He must rest. May I please invite you to call again on another occasion?"

Sambinsky rose, put his hands behind his back, and smiled graciously.

Formidable woman, thought Oscar. *Overcoming a police detective using only elegance and formality.*

"Goodbye, Inspector." She spoke warmly but firmly. "And goodbye, Mr. Orleans." Oscar hoped he had noticed an extra curl in her smile as she bid him farewell.

"This is nonsense," Sambinsky griped as they strode down the street toward his car.

"You must not feel bad, Inspector," Oscar said mildly. "You could hardly have arrested him. He is in a terrible state."

"Never mind his state," Kobi snorted. "There is much worse in store for him if he doesn't think fast. And think of his wife and baby."

"What will you do for them?"

"What can I do for them? He has to be willing to testify against Dumanovsky or at least give me enough that I can chase him down for the murder."

"Protective custody?"

"If I have enough to bring to the prosecutor, of course. But he has to talk. And he has to start telling the truth."

SEVENTEEN

Oscar could tell something was wrong. His eyes shot open, and he felt the adrenaline explode through his body.

Night terrors still woke him from time to time. Images of his best friend laid out on the slab at the Kinshasa morgue. Imagined replay of how he must have died. Horrible fantasies of being seized in the middle of the night by Colonel DuBest and cast into a pit like Joseph.

But now something was different. Something was moving in his room. He tried to remain silent and breathed through his nose.

There it was again. Oh Lord, thank G–d, he thought, calming himself. It was his mobile phone, vibrating on the hard wooden surface of his diminutive nightstand. He reached over and looked at it: 5:03. He didn't recognize the number, but it was someone here in Israel.

"Hello?" he answered, pushing himself up to sitting.

"Mr. Orleans, it's Lika Cone." Her Ukrainian accent was unmistakable. Oscar liked her immediately a little more for having introduced herself as Lika. "Mefake'ah Sambinsky wanted me to telephone you. He says you should come now. Can you come? I'll be downstairs in front of your house in three minutes."

Oscar figured there wasn't much to say to that except yes. He scrambled into a shirt and pants. He decided he might be forgiven for wearing an unpressed pair.

"We got a call around midnight," she said as she pressed the accelerator hard to the floor. The Kia Sorrento police cruiser screamed down Shabazi Street. Light was popping up from the horizon and beginning to sparkle against the buildings. But like the uniformed cadet, whose car she had commandeered for the journey and who sat beside him now in silence, Oscar was focusing on surviving the car ride. She might have scored low for bravery, but that didn't mean she didn't know how to be reckless. Why did all the officers in the Asylum Unit have to drive so damn fast? "Some unfortunate sanitation worker found them after eleven. Police called homicide. Homicide called the Chief Inspector. Chief Inspector called the Deputy. The Deputy remembered hearing us talking about similar guys yesterday in the pit at Salameh 18, and he called Sambinsky."

"I'm sorry, but what are we talking about?" Oscar gripped his arm rest.

"The dead guys," she said without irony.

"Yes, I understood you said homicide."

"*Nu?*"

"I mean, which dead guys, killed in whatever part of Tel Aviv to which you are piloting this police vehicle, have anything to do with me such that I am now sitting in the back seat at this unfortunate hour?" When tired and cranky, Oscar could, he realized, indeed sound like Hercule Poirot. "Surely there are no dead Africans at... where are we going?"

"On the way to Holon," she said. "Industrial section. No dead Africans. You'll see when we get there. Sambinsky is always up late. They called him before he'd gone to bed. He got there at one. I was there already. You should thank him. He told me to wait till five before I woke you up." Oscar was actually surprised and grateful. If they had been up all night, it would hardly do to complain about being rousted after five or six hours' sleep.

Bright spotlights were already mounted and connected to a mobile generator by the time they arrived. The sun was rising fast, but the homicide squad and forensic unit would want the dense illumination till they were finished. Four bodies were lined up under heavy black plastic on the concrete, which meant photographs had long been done and the bodies moved. Sambinsky was standing next to them, his right foot up on the bumper of a police van whose headlights were bathing the covered corpses in incandescence.

"You see this?" Sambinsky greeted Oscar. "Check it out." He gestured his chin to a young uniformed policewoman, who lifted back the flap of black plastic. The four bodies proved to be as distinct as they had been formless underneath it. Each was what you'd call either swarthy or pasty. Two had extensive tattooing. They were wearing revealing t-shirts and jeans that fitted extremely well or cargo pants that didn't.

"*Sapristi!*" Oscar covered his mouth.

"Yep. I'd bet you breakfast shekels these are the four hoods who assassinated our victim. They got it last night. Two of them were bound and gagged. Not the other two. All killed right in there." He pointed to the building, an ugly, rundown, iron-looking hulk, constructed for dirty missions of all kinds.

"What does that mean?" Oscar felt ill. The anxiety, the stress of death all around him, the pervasive menace of violence, and the sleeplessness. Not to mention the four bodies in front of him, impaled through the head or chest by bullets.

"See these two?" Sambinsky began. "Bound, gagged, one

shot to the head each. Those other two, a little different. This guy has been shot in the back of the head, not in the temple. His hands aren't tied, no gag on him when he was found. And this guy's been shot in the chest twice."

"I don't follow."

"I'd say they all came down here together, each with a different plan. First, these two tie up those two and kill them. Then the plan goes wrong."

"Who killed them?" Oscar asked, feeling lost.

"Whose plan?" Cone grinned.

"Acha! *Nachon*! Same question. So first these two kill the other two. Then someone shoots this guy in the back of his head. The last one is alarmed and lunges forward at him, but the shooter gets him in the chest twice."

"Seems to have gone according to someone's plan," Cone said. "Five guys show up. One walks out alive. Good plan."

"Yes. But whose?" Sambinsky pressed.

"You think Ruben Dumanovsky did this?" Oscar asked.

"You don't?" Sambinsky replied.

"We just saw him yesterday."

"Precisely. We went down to his office. Shook the tree about Sudan and his business there, and twelve hours later the men who killed a Sudanese who was known to be attempting a rendezvous with Dumanovsky show up murdered. Together. At the same time."

"If they were the same men," Cone clarified.

"Our blessed White City does not have so many gangland massacres," Sambinsky said. "I'm sure the technical guys will match their dimensions to the images of the men seen on the CCTV outside the Dolphinarium. No, no. These are the same thugs."

"So Dumanovsky murders these men just to make sure there

is no connection between him and the Shabbat murder." Oscar would not soon get used to the logic of hardened criminals.

"I think that's exactly what happened."

"*Nu?*" Oscar used the word sparingly. It was Yiddish, not Hebrew, so he did not feel entitled.

"Why don't I go arrest Dumanovsky right now?" Sambinsky understood what Oscar was thinking. "Look around you. It's not exactly CCTV central. Proving it was Dumanovsky is going to take some time. We'll have to start by canvassing the mob guys with photos of the victims. Find out who they were from the government databases. Homicide is going to have to lead. We're not big enough. Plus no one here looks like a refugee."

"So what's our job?" Oscar asked.

"Same as before, but now with even more urgency. We have to find out what Kuur knows. He's holding out on us. It's going to be bad for his health. Do you think you can get him to talk? Maybe you could go see him without me? Would that work?"

"I shall try, Inspector. I shall go see him later today. Perhaps he will be more open."

"Good. Meanwhile, we'll keep going on the Dumanovsky–Longokwo–Sudan connection. Get his dates and travel locked down and see if we can put the two men together more concretely."

EIGHTEEN

It made no sense to go back to bed, so Oscar asked the police cadet to drop him off at La Mer on Herbert Samuel. He could use an Americano and some time alone. On a weekday early morning the place was marvelous. He was often the only patron, and he could have the good fortune of watching the sea wake up to the sun. The mixture of open Mediterranean air on his skin and the hot Americano in his throat gave him great pleasure, and he could smoke a cigarillo if he chose, though he rarely chose. The memory of combined tobacco and coffee flavor was enough.

He was aware as he sat down of the adrenaline that had been pervading his body for the past few days. His stomach was churning, and his legs and arms were experiencing tiny tremors. Even his hands shook. He couldn't quite place it.

Perhaps he felt that somehow he, too, could be killed at any moment. The sad lot of the displaced person was to live with fear. Fear all the time. Fear that everything you cherished and labored to build could be taken away from you instantly and inexplicably. But something here was even worse than that. The sensation arising from the past days was acute. And somehow that rat bastard Ruben Dumanovsky was still alive and waltzing around Tel Aviv like an American teen on a summer internship.

Truly some people deserved to die.

Oscar closed his eyes. The faces of bad men – really bad men – who had entered his life over the decades paraded in front of him like ghosts. There were at least four on the same level as Dumanovsky. As far as Oscar knew, one had been killed, and the others were still alive and thriving.

The Rock, His work is perfect, for all His ways are justice; a G– d of faithfulness and without iniquity, righteous and just is He. The Rock, perfect in all His works. Who can say to Him, "What have You done?"

He drifted off to sleep.

"Mr. Orleans, Mr. Orleans." He heard a sweet feminine voice and then the gentle babble of a baby.

Oscar opened his eyes. Lily Kuur was seated at his table. He wiped his face with his hand and stumbled to his feet.

"Mrs. Kuur... " He didn't know what to say. "Excuse me."

"On the contrary, Mr. Orleans, please excuse me. It is I who have disturbed you."

"Not at all," he lied. She was very disturbing to him.

"We arrived almost twenty minutes ago. I have been waiting. But I shall soon have to go, and I did wish to speak with you about something that may be important."

The sun was bright in the sky, and the air had traded her morning chill for a sultry warmth. Oscar looked at his phone. He had been sleeping for almost an hour.

"Thank you for waking me, Mrs. Kuur," he said. "Otherwise I may have made quite an embarrassment of myself in front of the morning commuters." Somehow being in this woman's presence made him feel lighthearted. The baby was now staring at him, her fist in her mouth.

"Mr. Orleans, I came to find you here. All the Sudanese say that, when you are needed, this is where you will be." Oscar furrowed his eyebrows. He had heard that before. He wondered if being a creature of such obvious habit was good for him.

She drew up her chin and bounced her baby on her knee, preparing to speak.

"I must first say that I do not know if it is significant. But as I returned yesterday to my flat, I overheard you asking my husband about the poor young man's visit to the Dead Sea."

Oscar looked at her more intensely. She could not have helped noticing.

"Is that not correct?" she asked.

"It is correct."

"While I do not know about Kinga's visit to the Dead Sea, I can tell you that my husband has made many visits to the Dead Sea."

"*What?* I mean: Pardon me?"

"Many visits since I have known him. And always alone. Or at least always without me. And I believe he has been altogether alone."

"How often? How many such visits?"

"Since we were married last year, at least five or six. And before that, I am aware of two more during our courtship. It seems to me he had visited numerous times even before I met him."

"Why do you say that?"

"He usually goes for two or three nights. But sometimes for longer. He takes equipment and clothing suitable for overnight tent living. When he returns, his gear is rather filthy. His clothes require far too much attention." She smiled half-heartedly.

"Did he ever tell you what he is doing there?"

"In fact, at first he was vague even about his destination. Then I came upon bus tickets confirming he was traveling to a place called Ein Bokek, which I learned is the Dead Sea station. I asked him several times if I might join him on his journey as a pleasure trip. I have seen so little of this country. He has closed off the topic from discussion. He explained initially that he was needing some time alone and that the outdoors was no suitable place for a lady. Then later he grew impatient with me and simply forbade conversation about it."

"What do you think?"

"My first thoughts were of course what you would imagine. I suspected he had a woman in Ein Bokek." She looked ashamed, wistful. "No lady likes to admit such a possibility. Naturally, it would not be so out of the ordinary... " She turned her gaze outward to the sea. "He was never so very... enraptured of me, anyway. Not the way I had imagined, not the way I had hoped it would be. So I believed at first he must have had a liaison there."

The waitress brought an Americano for Oscar and asked her if she wanted anything. She shook her head.

"But then I realized this was almost certainly wrong. Why would he be meeting with a woman repeatedly in a tent at the Dead Sea? What kind of woman would agree to such a plan? And why, if he did, should his clothing all the time be filled with dirt and dust?" She looked at Oscar, her tone changing. "Then I found the tools."

"Tools? What tools?" Oscar's body was a bath of adrenaline. His heart was pumping with the knowledge that this was all somehow very damn important.

"A shovel. A pickaxe. Smaller shovels and trowels. He keeps them in a locker at the Jebena."

Oscar blinked, trying to piece it all together.

"I was helping clean the club early this year, and I thought I might find supplies in it. There was a collection of these implements bundled and stacked, and nothing else in there. Michael came into the back room, and he closed the locker right in front of me. He made a light joke of it and changed the subject. But when I next visited the club, there was a lock on the locker. His reaction prompted me to think. The dirt on the equipment was similar to the dirt he brings home on his clothes and shoes when he returns from the Dead Sea. So I concluded that he must bring them on his trips."

"That is most interesting, Mrs. Kuur. What do you make of it?"

"I am sure I do not know," she said, adjusting her baby to face her so she could rest on her bosom. "However, I believe my husband has been looking for a buried treasure."

"*What?*"

Lily breathed noisily through her teeth. "I know. It may sound... But I believe he is looking for something valuable that was buried near the Dead Sea some years ago."

"Why would you think that?"

"Some stray comments he has made over the years. A girlfriend notices. A wife knows. You can call it woman's intuition. No man can keep his intention clandestine from an observant wife for very long. If she cares about him, she will figure it out. Something he said here, something he said there. He told me a couple of times he hoped he would one day make me a rich woman. Once he was with a drinking friend in our parlor and, when they were quite in their cups, he said something about a 'secret buried in the hills.'" And he said on one occasion that he had been searching for something for many years. When you put it all together... " She looked at him. It was a logical proof.

"Thank you, Mrs. Kuur. This may be incredibly helpful to the police investigation."

"You see, Mr. Orleans, I love my husband. And I am a good

wife. I am very worried about him. I am afraid he is in terrible trouble, and I am anxious for the safety of our baby. If he will not help you, then I believe I must." She was gripping the corner of the table with her left hand.

"I understand completely. You have done the right thing. I assure you I shall do all I can to assist your husband and keep you and your baby safe. Now if you will please excuse me, I have some urgent following up to do. Here is my mobile number. And please give me yours."

Lily Kuur carefully recited her phone number, rose, and carried Nellie down the *tayelet*. Oscar admired from behind for a few steps, and then started dialing on his phone. His mind was reeling with urgent things he had to do. First of which, he had to call Kobi.

"Hello, boychik," Kobi answered quickly. "*Ma kore?*" *What's up?* "You haven't already talked to Kuur, have you?"

"Inspector Sambinsky, please listen carefully. I have something to tell you."

NINETEEN

"I think I may just kill him myself," Kobi said as Oscar arrived at the lobby of Salameh 18. He looked at least half serious.

Though Oscar had been paid as a police liaison for the better part of a decade, and though the Police Headquarters personnel knew his face well, he still had no official law enforcement ID. A cop had to meet him downstairs every time and escort him to the second floor. He had a semi-official desk, which he almost never used, but no badge, no business card, no email address, no status. Just a paycheck and familiarity. It was a casual if unintentional bureaucratic reminder of his statelessness. *You can sit around here sometimes if you want, but you are not free to move about or to call yourself one of us.*

"Come up. Angelika is waiting for you. She has theories."

Sambinsky had nearly lost his mind when Oscar relayed the new information on the phone. He had told him to come to headquarters after lunch so they could run some of the new data down first. But it was clear from Kobi's face that the wound of Pastor Kuur's ongoing omissions was still fresh.

"Go ahead," Sambinsky instructed Angelika as they reached the pit and assembled at an open table. She started immediately.

"First, we have confirmation of Dumanovsky's travel to Sudan. Every trip we had surmised was to Sudan was, in fact, to Sudan. He also went to Angola once and to South Africa another time. But Sudan has been his main destination in Africa."

"Okay, okay." Kobi circled his hand at the wrist to indicate she should move on.

"Second, I had some uniforms go through more CCTV from Hatachana Merkazit. They found our victim on his outbound bus ride. He went to the Dead Sea a little more than three weeks before he returned."

"Truly?" Oscar's mouth gaped. He felt his tongue brush his molars reflexively. A thought flickered through his brain nearly too fast for him to catch it.

"Good use of the uniforms, right?" Sambinsky asked, deliberately missing the point. "She's getting the hang of it."

"He must have brought a lot of food." It was all Oscar could muster. He didn't feel much like humor at the moment. Something he couldn't place was causing him pain. But Angelika smiled and Sambinsky gave a snort. They thought it was funny enough.

"Third, I've been trying to piece together what you told Inspector Sambinsky. Obviously, if Pastor Michael Kuur has been digging around the Dead Sea with shovels and axes, then that's what the victim Kinga was doing out there. And if Kuur has been looking for buried treasure, then the victim Kinga was, too."

"Indisputable, Sherlock."

"So the questions are: One, did Kuur and Kinga collaborate on the expedition to the Dead Sea? Two, if not, did Kuur at least know that the victim Kinga was going out there? Three, if not, how did Pastor Michael Kuur and the victim come to know, separately, that there might be buried treasure somewhere near the Dead Sea?"

"They heard it from the same source." Oscar supplied the answer almost like he was asking a question.

Angelika nodded. She had come to the same conclusion. "Who do you think?" She winked at him. For a fresh member of the Asylum Unit with the lowest scores for bravery ever recorded, she was acquiring her confidence fast.

"The first Kinga told them?" Oscar was asking this time.

No one said anything, but Angelika bobbed her head slowly.

"Motive," Sambinsky said.

"I don't follow," Oscar replied. He felt lost.

"Kinga I tells Kuur there is a horde of valuables buried at the Dead Sea. He probably brought it with him from Africa and buried it himself for safekeeping. Most likely it was a scheduled shipment for the deal with Dumanovsky."

Oscar picked it up. "The first Kinga of eight years ago transports a stash of gold to Israel as part of the longstanding arrangement between his father Father Longokwo and Ruben Dumanovsky. They have a dispute. To secure his collateral, Kinga brings the gold to the Dead Sea and buries it somewhere. Before he disappears, he informs his father – and perhaps even his child brother – of his stratagem. He also informs Pastor Kuur. He confides in his countryman, in a Christian, in a man of the cloth, like his father. He does not reveal the exact location of the prize. But he tells him the broad strokes."

"Then he disappears from the face of the earth," Cone said, crossing her arms.

"Which we no longer believe Dumanovsky had anything to do with?" Oscar asked.

"On the contrary," Sambinsky answered almost joyously. "Motives are coming out of our ears! If Kinga I is holding out on Dumanovsky, burying his gold deep in the mud around the Dead

Sea, then Dumanovsky has every reason in the world to kill him. But so does Kuur. If Kuur decides he wants the treasure for himself, he kills Kinga I. But he kills him too soon! Too soon! He doesn't know the exact location of the gold. So he keeps looking for years, out there on his own, digging through the muck, lying to his own wife about it."

"Exactly," Cone shakes her head. It occurred to Oscar for a second that she might be more offended by Kuur's lying to his wife.

"Now comes Kinga II," Sambinsky continued. "Kuur wins his trust, referring to the memory of his dead brother. The young man has no cause to doubt him. Kuur tries to persuade him to reveal the location of the treasure. Kinga II won't. Or he can't, because he doesn't know. If he did, why would he spend three weeks at the Dead Sea looking for it? He'd have gone out there, retrieved it, and come back. Kuur gets frustrated. He kills the young man."

"But you already said—" Oscar objected.

"I know what I said. The four dead white men who killed the victim on Shabbat didn't work for Kuur. It is still my opinion. I agree with myself."

"So?"

"So, Dumanovsky." Kobi thrust his forefinger in the air. "Let's say Kuur tells Dumanovsky about Kinga II's search for the treasure. Or, take Kuur out of it altogether. Suppose Dumanovsky figured out that Kinga II would be looking for his brother's treasure. Or, maybe, just as plausible, Kinga II told Dumanovsky he would look for it and trade it for something he wanted. Maybe the Shabbat victim Kinga even asked for help looking for it."

"Or Dumanovsky offered to help him, whether he asked for the help or not," Cone said.

"Yep, that sounds more likely."

"Then why would Dumanovsky have him killed?" Oscar asked. "If Dumanovsky needs him to find the treasure, why murder him?"

Kobi drummed his fingertips on the table. "That is a good question."

"Maybe they found it," Cone answered quietly.

"Okay." Sambinsky tried it on. "They found it. Dumanovsky doesn't want to share. He has the child Kinga II killed so he can keep it for himself. Could be."

"Or maybe Kinga won't cooperate with him?" Oscar suggested.

"Meaning?"

"Meaning that Kinga refuses to cooperate with Dumanovsky in the search for his brother's treasure. Dumanovsky grows angry and frustrated, and he has the young man assassinated," Oscar said.

"I can see it," Sambinsky nodded, his lips pursed broadly and turned downwards to indicate they should stay open to various theories for now.

"Maybe it was a mistake." Cone's expression revealed she felt she had just stumbled onto something.

"A mistake? Of what kind? Kinga made a mistake in confiding in Dumanovsky?" Sambinsky asked.

"A mistake to kill him. Maybe Dumanovsky's men killed him because they thought they were fulfilling their boss's wishes. But he actually doesn't want him dead. He just wants him to hand over the treasure if he gets his hands on it."

"And, for their sins, they get killed by him—" Sambinsky turned it over out loud. "Could be, could be. What else?"

"Perhaps the young man Kinga confronts the mobster Dumanovsky about his long-lost brother, or perhaps about a long-overdue payment from his father's era. But he doesn't mention the trove at all. Dumanovsky has a reason to get rid of him – he threatens to be a nuisance if he stays alive – and he has no reason to ensure his safety. He may not even suspect that the young Kinga knows of any buried treasure at the Dead Sea."

"That would probably satisfy Occam," Sambinsky agreed.

"It might also explain one other clue we have collected," Oscar said.

"Which is...?" Sambinsky and Cone looked at him intently.

"Dumanovsky's reaction when you mentioned that the victim was carrying gold on his person," Oscar answered.

"Interesting!" Sambinsky sat up. "You mean that, the way Dumanovsky heard it, Kinga II was toting a large amount of gold around him, the kind of gold you'd find at a buried treasure site, instead of a small nugget in the cavity of his mouth like you'd secret away for a personal emergency."

"Yes. All of that," Oscar said.

"What precisely did you say to Dumanovsky?" Cone asked the police question.

Sambinsky looked up at the ceiling, trying to recall. "Oscar is right. I referenced gold Kinga was carrying around Tel Aviv. Not an amount."

"You didn't say anything about a cavity in his tooth? Didn't mention his mouth?" Cone asked further.

"No, I don't think I did. Oscar?"

"You did not. He did not."

"So, when we inform him that Kinga has gold on his person, Dumanovsky is caught off guard." Sambinsky wanted to lay it out explicitly. "He wonders if the Shabbat victim Kinga had found a hoard of treasure at the Dead Sea and brought it back with him to Tel Aviv. He realizes he made a terrible mistake in having him killed before accessing his secrets. He wonders why his men found no gold on him when they shot him to death at the Dolphinarium. Or he suspects that they did find gold on him and kept it for themselves. He grows furious that they could be so incompetent or that they have tried to cheat him. Take your pick. He kills them, too." A smile grew on Sambinsky's face as he recited the steps. "It fits, Oscar. It fits!" Angelika grinned, as well.

"And may I say –" Oscar became just a touch more formal to cover his incipient pride – "it could help explain what happened to Pastor Michael Kuur after Dumanovsky learned about the gold the Shabbat victim Kinga had on him."

"Hercule! You are *ze real thing*!" Sambinsky exclaimed.

"What?" Cone asked. She wanted to be sure.

"Dumanovsky learns about the gold and figures Kuur has been holding out on him. Surely, he thinks, if anyone knows that Kinga II had found his missing brother's buried treasure, it was Kuur. So Dumanovsky beats him up, threatens his life and his family, and demands to know what Kuur knows."

"What does Kuur know?" Oscar asked.

"I don't know. How could I? He wasn't fucking telling us anything."

"This version feels true. It feels right." Cone stood up and paced. She sat back down, this time at the edge of the table. Sambinsky looked at her face and drew confidence from hers. Oscar knew that sometimes that was all there was to be had in Kobi's job: an intuition that a certain explanation of the accumulated facts and surmises was the best possible one. And it was often enough to form the basis of an investigation, if not always a conviction.

"Well, I can tell you one thing for sure," Kobi said, standing up. "I have officially had enough of this pastor's shit."

TWENTY

Sambinsky parked the car on HaGalil Street and leapt out, crossing the road before Oscar or Cone had managed to close their own doors. They scurried after him. He was knocking on the Sudanese-flagged door by the time they started climbing the staircase. When Mefake'ah Sambinsky was on a tear, it was best to stay out of his way. His body language switched from pudgy Jew to prizefighter, and his temper could punch through a concrete wall.

Sambinsky knocked again, harder. No answer. He removed his pistol from its holster. Both Cone and Oscar stepped back from the landing in alarm. Kobi used the butt of the gun to bang the door even more loudly. The paint chipped away from one of the points of the flag's star. Oscar felt worried.

"Michael! Mrs. Kuur! This is the police! Answer your door now!" Sambinsky yelled.

Still nothing. Sambinsky rapped one more time then holstered his gun. "No one home." He looked at them.

"Jebena," Oscar suggested.

Kobi was flying down the stairs before they could turn

around. They made chase as he barreled down HaGalil and onto Neve Sha'anan Street. The day was not too hot, but Kobi was already starting to sweat through his shirt. "Keep up, Cone!" he shouted back at them. He wanted to have a visible police presence as he burst through the doors of the private club.

And he did burst through them.

"Everybody out!" he shouted as soon as he saw Michael Kuur sitting on his usual throne. Cone was right on his heels, and Oscar behind her. "Now!" Sambinsky waved his badge, and the handful of Africans sitting on cushions and drinking guhwah climbed to their feet and walked past them out the door wordlessly. Lily was not present. The old lady minding the club the other day peeked her head out from the back room and then gathered up her scarf and left. Only Kuur remained, sitting in his elevated chair in his empty room like a king without a court.

Sambinsky marched up to him like he was going to deliver a death blow, and Kuur recoiled in fear. Half his face was still covered in bandages, but the other half showed terror and the pain shooting through his body as he drew back his limbs to protect himself.

"You piece of shit, you better start talking now, I mean now, and I mean tell me everything, or you better believe I'm going to charge you with being an accessory to murder, and then I'm going to start making your life miserable. I'm going to have you on the first fucking flight out of here to Juba. I'm going to give your name to Interpol so you can never leave that shithole again in your life, and then I'm going to make personally sure Ruben Dumanovsky knows it was you fingered him to the police, so your helpless wife and daughter better pray he doesn't hold a grudge against your family." He loomed over Kuur's chair, placing his hands on the armrests and his face just centimeters from his. He felt his spittle land on the man's cheek.

Oscar stepped back toward the entrance door. Sambinsky had been like an explosion. He felt he had to move away from the blast radius. He was shocked by the ugliness of it. He knew his friend well enough – he thought he knew his friend well enough – to feel confident he would not visit such a horror on a man's family. But he had never before seen this kind of nasty display. And to go straight to the jugular vein of what a man worried about most? Deportation, murder of his wife and child. It was thuggery. *And what does that make me?* he wondered. Oscar looked at Angelika. Her arms were crossed at the elbows and her stance a confident military suspect-gazing posture. That was her army and police training. She was giving no quarter. When those guys wanted to dehumanize someone, they knew how to do it.

"Come on, you sack of shit! Speak! You lying fuck! You've got ten seconds to help me or you're going to be on the next boat to the fucking Sahara desert."

Oscar was glad Kobi hadn't said anything racist. In these moments, people were apt to say things they might not mean. But it would be hard to overlook if he did.

"I... I... " Kuur started.

"Come on, you lousy fuck. Right now. Don't even try to pretend you can't speak. You can talk perfectly when you want to. Out with it."

"My family... "

"Right now I don't give a Cossack's assfuck about your family. All I care about is one dead African and the fact that every single road in this investigation leads to you, you mongrel piece of shit."

Oscar winced. *Mongrel. What did he mean by mongrel? Please, Kobi, no more.* Angelika turned away from the chair and toward the door into Jebena. She had sensed something. Oscar saw two Sudanese leaning against the windows on the outside, trying to peer in. They scrambled away, and Cone resumed her battle stance.

Sambinsky changed his tone as fast as he had initiated it. He spoke firmly but quietly.

"We know about the buried treasure, Kuur. We know you've been looking for it. You realize that marks you with a giant neon sign that says 'motive.'"

Kuur looked horrified. "You know about the treasure?" he said feebly.

"You better believe it."

"Then you must know how important it is that we find it."

It was one of those moments when you could feel the air change. Something new was about to be revealed. Oscar had been in this very room late at night some years ago when he had learned the vital importance of stillness on these occasions. He froze reflexively, not wanting to mess it up. He could barely catch Angelika in the corner of his eye. She had stepped closer to Kuur's chair. Sambinsky didn't move at all.

"What do you mean?" Kobi's voice was all gravel.

"We have to find it before anyone else does."

"Who is we?" Sambinsky asked.

"The Sudanese, of course." Kuur's pained look was now mixed with confusion. "I had nothing to do with that poor boy's death," he said. "If you know about the treasure, you must understand that."

"You're trying to tell me the reason you didn't have anything to do with the Shabbat murder is that you had some kind of a shared patriotic responsibility with the victim for the treasure? Give me a break. Of all the bullshit I've ever heard from a perp." Sambinsky stood up, his body language betraying his actual point of view. He was mulling what it could be that he did not yet know.

"Mefake'ah, if I had killed him, we would never be able to

retrieve it. Of course I did not kill him." Kuur was still looking terrorized, but he could tell the detective was listening.

Sambinsky turned his head to look at Oscar, which gave him the permission he needed.

"Michael, tell us about the gold," Oscar said. "Tell us what you know."

"You mean you do not know?" Kuur asked, his eyes wide open.

"Perhaps," Oscar said.

Sambinsky interrupted. "We know your friend Kinga from eight years ago showed up with a treasure of some kind, buried it at the Dead Sea, and then got killed by someone who wanted it. Then a couple months ago a younger man with the same name shows up and goes looking for it in the same place, the same place you've been looking for it for years. And then he comes back to Tel Aviv, and a few days later he's dead."

Kuur breathed in slowly and exhaled at the same pace.

"Then I am afraid, Inspector, that there is a great deal you do not know."

TWENTY-ONE

M any years ago, a great queen from a distant land visited Jerusalem. She brought with her unimaginable treasure. There is no clear record of her name, but she is remembered throughout history by the name of her realm. The Bible referred to her only as the Queen of Sheba. The queen's journey took seven years. Her expedition changed the course of her life and of history. For it was while she was here that she fell in love with Solomon, King of Israel.

We may never know why she traveled to Israel. Most stories of their courtship tell that she came to see a man known to be close to G–d. Many stories agree that she was taken with the rumors of his immeasurable wisdom. She came to test him with riddles. Perhaps she came to win his love. Many accounts suggest that she remarked, after her arrival, upon how happy his wives must have been.

For reasons of statecraft or of commerce, or perhaps anticipating her love, the queen prepared sumptuous riches to be shared with King Solomon. In advance of her retinue, she sent *train upon train of camel and horse laden with jewels, spices, silks, and gold. She brought even more with her to present upon her arrival.*

We do not know the full extent of her relationship with Solomon. But it was passionate. When she left again for Sheba, she took with her a child. This was the offspring of her union with the king.

Perhaps it was the advent of this child that prompted her to leave. Perhaps she intended to return to Israel one day. But she never came back.

Some scholars believe that the queen hailed from Arabia. Ancient sources tell us she was the queen of Egypt, Ethiopia, and more. This majestic woman ruled over a vast stretch of the arc that describes the tracts west of the Nile River to the reaches east of Yemen. And it is from all of her lands, and from even her neighboring lands, that she cultivated and collected gifts to bring to Solomon. She brought him fine, precious wood from the north, silk from the east, and rare spice from the south. And from the west, she brought gold.

Heaps and heaps of gold. The ancient world had never seen so much gold transported at once. Contemporary traditions recount sums of gold that would fill cargo ships. Hundreds upon hundreds of talents preceded and followed the Queen of Sheba and her train. Even for this king of wealth, her gifts were fabulous.

And there were jewels besides. She brought with her necklaces, rings, ornaments, baubles, and crowns, assembled by the greatest craftsmen in her empire. The gold was mixed from the deepest, richest sources in the land and molded and refined into breathtaking creations by the most exceptional jewelers from the farthest corners of her realm. There were many skilled workers in her empire, and there were many rich mines. But the greatest goldworkers in all her dominion, and the best gold mined in all her lands, were to be found in what is today known as South Sudan.

The progenitors of the tribe who have been known for centuries as the Toposa were the masters of the deepest mines in the world, protecting rich seams of purest gold that they maintained as the most closely guarded secrets of their people. They likewise shrouded a custom, already ancient in the queen's own lifetime, of meticulous and splendid goldsmithing. Their work was known for its intricacy and delicacy. They believed symmetry and complexity were the highest forms of their art, far worthier of their unadulterated, noble metal than the mere luster favored by other nations.

The most exquisite form of jewel they made was a kind of layered chain mail, all gold, heavy enough to move with the body of the person lucky enough to wear it on his arm or her breast but light enough never to deform the links. And the most exquisite of these creations ever assembled was the one commissioned by the Queen of Sheba for her journey. It was composed of long, threaded strands, woven together like silk and spider webs; seamless cords of identical loops, hooping into one another like symbols of infinity, revealing no indication that they had ever been soldered; still more chains of ovals and circles of the same and varying sizes; and then tiny, nearly invisible skeins of gold, binding the strands together so they might flow on her figure in unison while she moved.

The beauty of this piece was instantly legendary. It is said that when the Toposa goldsmiths revealed it, her ladies in waiting fell to their knees and began to cry. When outstretched, it was longer than a grown man's arm. From top to bottom, it was as tall as the stem of a flowering hibiscus, as a token of regard for the makers' homeland. Though it was so vast, when turned on its side it was barely visible, so narrow and fine was their work. And when the queen tried it on, her court was moved to cover their mouths in awe, as it fit her shape exactly and without weighing down the grace of her movements. The piece was so beautiful, and it matched her person so perfectly, that it was said to make the sound of starlight as she walked like a cat around her throne room.

It was a jewel of her own devising, meant to assist her in the greatest seduction ever recorded. Her artisans from South Sudan exceeded even her dreams. As a reward, and to safeguard the delicate object, she brought with her to Jerusalem a delegation of the best goldsmiths of their tribe.

The piece was a wrap made of gold, a precious metal scarf to be worn around the queen's hips. It was an invitation and a fence, a persuasion and a hurdle, a treasure and an armor. Nothing could have been more fit to drive a king mad with lust. It could not have worked her intended magic better.

The legend of the queen's encounter with Solomon has been told many times. But the best accounts of what transpired include mention of a superb chain she wore around her hips when she met him. It is reputed that, when they consummated their passion, she wore only this exquisite chain to bed.

Most of the treasures the Queen of Sheba brought to Jerusalem she gave to Solomon to keep. But not all. Her personal jewels, worn to ornament her body, she took with her as she left Solomon's court. Perhaps it was only natural that she should.

But not all of this private treasure made it back to her kingdom. It is well documented that she intended to return one day to Jerusalem. We do not know why she planned to come back. Perhaps after the child attained a certain age, she hoped to return triumphantly in a union of her love and of the two kingdoms. Or perhaps she fled to protect the safety of her baby from Solomon's envious wives. Once her offspring with Solomon was hardy enough, she might come back to battle them and claim the throne of Israel for him. Perhaps we will never know. But the legend of her voyage is that she left her heart in Israel and wanted to see her love again before she grew old.

There is more.

The Toposa have preserved the secret of her departure for three thousand years. The story has been handed down from father to son in an unbroken line. Just as Ethiopia remembers her own rulers' descent from that child born of their queen and Solomon, and just as the Yoruba have maintained the memory of their connection to the queen's lineage, so, too, have the Toposa remembered their role in that incredible journey. Relying on closely guarded oral histories, they have maintained a precise record of the queen's retreat from Jerusalem.

It was an unhappy farewell. The Queen of Sheba was reluctant to leave, and King Solomon was equally reluctant to see her go. She pledged to return. He pledged to receive her.

The queen made a plan, in part as a valuable token of her determination to come back. She entrusted her goldsmiths with burying a portion of her personal hoard in the desert cliffs near the Dead Sea. The goldsmiths trudged off in darkness, selected a cave, and buried the gold, including the queen's prized hip chain, deep in the ground. In this way, she ensured she would return and be as bedazzling for her king as ever before. She swore her Toposa jewelers to secrecy, and they went back to their own homeland with the secret intact.

Since that time, the Toposa have safeguarded the mystery of that ancient queen. Though they do not know the exact location of the cave, they are aware it is located in the desert hills above the Dead Sea. Their secrecy has been maintained by the remote and close-knit history of their tribe. Their people have been resistant to outsiders for millennia. The queen could have chosen no better nation to safeguard her treasure.

Of course, the Queen of Sheba never returned to Israel. She never saw Jerusalem or King Solomon again. She never retrieved her hoard. The progenitors of the Toposa in South Sudan never had occasion to revisit the land of the Jews, not even in the era of the Abyssinian Empire.

Her gold must still be there, waiting to be found.

Somewhere in the desert near the Dead Sea lies the greatest treasure of Solomon's times, and the greatest jewel and most powerful symbol of romantic and national seduction ever created.

TWENTY-TWO

"Holy shit," Officer Cone exhaled. She was sitting on the cushions closest to Pastor Kuur's large chair.

Oscar and Sambinsky were speechless. They, too, had found themselves sitting down during the retelling. It was as if a world had been opened up for them, a world requiring the full attention and energy of their bodies and minds to ingest.

Kuur closed his eyes. The story had exhausted him. He swallowed. Oscar noticed Kuur's discomfort and wanted to get him water. But he was immobilized by the encounter with the mystery of the queen's treasure and wanted urgently to sit where he was and listen to what his brain might tell him next. He forgave himself the indulgence and promised himself to rise and get Kuur some water in a few minutes if no one else had.

"You have been looking for that golden hip scarf...?" Kobi asked in a near whisper.

"In one way or another, I have been searching near the Dead Sea since a young man named Kinga first told me about it eight years ago."

"Truly?" Oscar asked, amazed.

"No. Not truly," Kuur allowed. "At first I did not believe him. He told me this tale – he told me in confidence... " Kuur covered his eyes and choked back a sudden wave of tears. "That poor boy." They waited for him to compose himself. "You see, he told me in confidence of this unimaginable treasure. He told me in such great detail. He urged me – implored me – to join him in the search. But I thought it was just a young man's fantasy or some tribal lore he was taking too seriously. He was, in his way, a most imaginative and passionate young man."

Kobi looked up, affected, perhaps, by Kuur's memory of the unfortunate soul who had entered his life, however briefly, nearly a decade earlier.

"When did you start believing him?" Kobi asked.

Kuur breathed out through his mouth slowly. "When it was too late." He went quiet.

"How so? Come on, Pastor, you must tell us now." Kobi's tone was gentle, almost tender. He tapped Kuur's knee with his palm.

"When I refused him help, he went to Ruben Dumanovsky."

Oscar sighed audibly. Kuur looked up. Shame smothered his face like gauze.

"I know, Oscar. You are right. My refusal has been a font of remorse and distance for years. I do not know if the young man Kinga approached Dumanovsky because I refused or if he was planning on doing so anyway. There was a long history between his family and Mr. Dumanovsky. He was inclined to trust him. You see, Mr. Dumanovsky had done business previously with his father, Father Longokwo." He looked up expectantly at the others. "Ah." He nodded. "You know that already. What a small world we find and make," he said to himself. "To my everlasting shame, what I refused, Dumanovsky agreed to do. The assistance I could have provided was substituted by the kind of assistance a monster like Dumanovsky would furnish."

"Which was what? Be specific," Kobi said.

"Of course, there were more resources. Tools, food, supplies. I believe Dumanovsky even went out there to the desert himself. But without question, Dumanovsky demanded much of the young man. He grew afraid."

"How do you know that?" Kobi pressed.

"Is it not obvious?" Kuur asked pleadingly.

"Not good enough," Kobi said quickly. "You have to tell us more this time. You can't hold back."

Just then a thought flashed again through Oscar's mind. It had come before, and now it came flying back for just an instant. He concluded that Sambinsky was perhaps missing the point, but he held his tongue.

"Kinga returned from the desert during this search. He returned to Tel Aviv just for a couple of days on a couple of occasions, to resupply and rest. When I saw him, he complained bitterly of the desert, of the search, and of the conditions. But most of all he complained of Dumanovsky. He said he was not the man his father had known. He said he was brutal, a slave driver, abusive and tormenting and threatening. He was as afraid of finding the treasure as he was of failing to find it."

"He was afraid of what?"

Kuur waved his hand gently as if trying to conjure a memory. "It was eight years ago, Inspector... "

Kobi nodded. "Go on."

"Perhaps the end result will tell you enough," Kuur continued. "After his last visit to Tel Aviv, Kinga departed again for the desert with fresh supplies. He never came back."

"What do you mean?" Cone asked.

"I mean he never came back from the desert."

"You mean he's buried out there somewhere? Dumanovsky killed him?"

"I can only imagine so," Kuur said, resignation and regret hanging in his voice like humidity.

"So, actually, all this time...?" Oscar let it trail off deliberately.

"I have been looking for his remains," Kuur confirmed.

"Holy shit," Cone said again.

"Not the gold?" Sambinsky asked.

"I told you. I didn't believe there was any."

There was a pause. The room was puzzling it out.

"Until when, Michael?" Oscar sounded serious.

"Until Saturday night, when you told me of the gold inside the cavity of his mouth."

"*Mon dieu,*" Oscar breathed. "So it is true."

"It must be," Kuur replied.

"Wait a second. What?" Kobi was catching up.

Oscar put it together. "The gold we found in the Shabbat victim's mouth was not smuggler's gold he had brought with him overland. Nor was it gold his brother had brought eight years ago. It is Sudanese gold, just as the laboratory confirmed. But it has been lying undisturbed in the desert above the Dead Sea for three thousand years. Until our young Kinga found it in the past few weeks."

"You mean...?" Cone touched her face at the jawline reflexively.

"The dental injury was self-inflicted. Out there in the desert. He had to find a way to convey a small sample safely. Isn't that right, Michael?" Oscar asked.

"I think it must be. I don't believe he had any such wound in his mouth before he departed for Ein Bokek. He was staying in our flat. I think I would have noticed. It would have been too painful to conceal."

"Excruciating," Cone said softly, wincing.

"Motherfuck," Kobi said out loud, to no one in particular.

"Excuse me. I'm just getting the picture. So let's fast forward. You look in vain for the remains of Kinga I for years. Then what happens? One day the so-called Kinga II shows up at your door?"

"More or less."

"When?"

"Two months ago? I can't be more precise right now, but my wife might recollect the date."

"He asked for a place to stay?"

"I offered. Our flat is modest, but it is better than many alternatives. He also slept here in Jebena one or two nights."

"Okay. So then what?"

"He wanted to know what had happened to his brother. He said his father had died a miserable man, knowing, suspecting that some accident or evil had befallen him. His father's dying wish had been to hear from his son one last time. But he never did."

"So this new young man, the younger brother, he came to Israel why? For revenge? To learn what had happened? To find the gold?"

"He believed his brother and Dumanovsky had found the gold and that Dumanovsky had turned on him and killed him to keep it for himself."

"Really? Why did he believe that?"

"Because his father had told Dumanovsky about the gold some years back."

"*Dumanovsky knew about the gold?*"

"Insofar as anyone knew, insofar as Father Longokwo would have been able to tell him, and his own son – yes."

"What the hell does that mean, Kuur? Will you please stop with the riddles? This is no fucking time." Sambinsky rose to his feet.

"I apologize, Inspector. I mean only that Father Longokwo likely did not know the exact location of the treasure. If he told

Dumanovsky about it, he would have been able to point only to a general direction. I doubt Dumanovsky believed him. Not until Father Longokwo sent his own son to look for it eight years ago, anyway."

"How did the young man killed on Shabbat get the impression his brother and Dumanovsky had found the gold?" Kobi was pacing now.

"Probably just a boy's idea of what must have happened. Nothing more."

"Certainly that would have been a motive for Dumanovsky: find the gold, kill the kid, keep the gold. What did you tell him?"

"I told him it was possible but unlikely."

"Why? Dammit, Kuur. Spit."

"Because Dumanovsky has been hounding me about the gold ever since."

"What does that mean, Michael? Can you be more specific?" Oscar asked gently, interjecting, wanting to avoid letting Kobi get further riled up.

"Dumanovsky has never let the idea go that maybe there was a vast treasure out there in the desert. He has asked me about it, pushed me about it, cajoled me, threatened me, joked about it for years. When I have asked him what happened to the young man Kinga eight years ago, his story has changed. At first he brushed it off, saying the boy must have found the gold and disappeared back to Africa or to Europe. Then he said the boy must have died of thirst in the desert, as if a Toposa would know how to die of thirst in the desert. Bah! On other occasions he has simply brushed it off or changed the subject. But he has never stopped insisting that whatever gold is out there is his, belongs to him, that he paid for the young man's expedition and was out there with him searching, too, so he must get the lion's share if ever it is found. He is mad about it. A crazy person. The calm exterior comes off when he wants to remove it, and he becomes a creature of great violence."

"No shit." Kobi couldn't help himself.

"Dumanovsky is of course aware that I have made many trips out there to the caves. He believes that I have been looking for the gold. Periodically he will visit and check on my circumstances, looking for signs that I have suddenly come into great wealth. He reminds me with explicit and veiled threats that, should I ever locate the treasure, it is his."

"Why lie? Why did you lie to us?" Kobi asked.

"Look at me!" Pastor Kuur shouted. "I have been living in fear for my future since leaving my homeland and coming to this country. I have been living in fear for my life since Dumanovsky came into it. How could I explain it to you? I hate that man. Anything I said to connect me to the boy and then on to Dumanovsky could result in... Ever since you left here I have been regretting even mentioning that the victim was searching for Dumanovsky. I thought maybe you could connect him to the murder without knowing I was mixed up with him, too. I thought I could get rid of him. It was foolish. Look at me." He put his hand to his forehead and rubbed it.

"All right." Kobi rubbed his own face, too. "So let's close the loop. Dumanovsky learns that Kinga II the Shabbat victim had gold on his person—"

"From you. He learned that from you."

"True. I apologize."

"Mefake'ah," Cone said.

"Yes?" He turned to face her.

"Go back. The Shabbat victim Kinga comes to Israel. He believes his brother and Dumanovsky found the gold and that Dumanovsky had him killed. You tell him it's unlikely. Then what?" Oscar was impressed. She was indeed more thorough than her boss.

Kuur's face expressed the same. "He wanted to confront Dumanovsky," he said. "You know young men. They are the same everywhere."

"Did he?" Cone said.

"No. I persuaded him that Dumanovsky was a dangerous man and that it was very unlikely he had found the gold, given his ongoing interest in my finding it."

"So then what?"

"Then he did the other thing a young man would do. He set off for the desert to look for it himself."

"Not for his brother's body."

"I did not have the heart to tell him what I suspected about the brother's final resting place. Perhaps he suspected. Perhaps he set out to look for the remains, too. I offered him some tools. He accepted."

"Did you go with him?"

"No. Since the baby—"

"Then he came back last week?" Cone was on a steady tear.

"Yes."

"Had he returned before?"

"Not that I know."

"What happened?"

"He said he wanted to see Dumanovsky. I tried to dissuade him. He was immovable. His demeanor had changed. He was more determined, more mature, a boy quickly becoming a man. The ancient story of a young man gone out on a quest and returned a different one. He did not look the same. He did not stand the same. He did not breathe the same. Still I refused to bring him to Dumanovsky. But I believe he was able to find another means of locating him."

"Then what?"

"Then you told me he was killed."

"When was the last time you saw him?"

"Two or three days before Shabbat. He was not staying with me. He was not staying here at Jebena, either. I do not know where he slept. He kept to himself. He suddenly possessed a difficult pride. He was almost condescending. It is not unusual for a young man. Now of course I understand better why. He may have been bursting with a secret that had been successfully kept by his people since the time of the First Temple. He was the discoverer of an ancient lost national patrimony. If only he had not sought out Dumanovsky but instead gone back home or told an authority."

"Where is it now?" Kobi changed the tone.

"What?"

"The gold, Kuur. The treasure. Where is it?"

"Your guess is as good as mine. As you can see from my injuries, you are not the only one who has been asking."

Kobi breathed out through his nose. He knew Kuur might say it again. Even if Kuur said it one hundred more times, he knew he deserved it.

"So let's go back to that. Dumanovsky learns – from me – that the Shabbat victim Kinga II had gold on him. Then what?"

"He came to see me."

"Where?"

"Here." Kuur waved his arm around Jebena. "He sent a man in the afternoon to tell me he wished to see me that evening at nine. I was scared, but it was not so unusual. I didn't know why he wanted to meet, after all. After supper with my family, I returned here at 8:45 to open up and prepare to meet him."

"What happened?" Kobi asked, moving in front of Kuur to take up his field of view as Cone stepped sideways behind Kuur's chair so she could open her flipbook unnoticed.

"As I was unlocking the door, someone grabbed me from behind. A hood of some kind was thrown over my head." He gesticulated his arms and hands to show how it had come down over his face. "Before I knew what was happening, I had been thrust inside the Jebena, and I was on the floor, somewhere there, suffering terrible blows with hard sticks and kicks from heavy shoes. I was told to shut up and not cry out. It was a most miserable punishment. Out of fear for my life, I did not dare raise an alarm or shout in pain. I managed to maintain my silence. To hear the blows fall and to hear them crunch bone in this hollow, empty, reverberating room, and to hear nothing else but grunts and hard breathing of men in an ecstasy of violence, and to realize that these blows on bone were blows on my bone, was to feel the injuries doubly. I believed I was there to die."

"How did you know—" Kobi started.

"Because I heard his voice. After they stopped, he asked me questions. It was Dumanovsky's voice. There is no mistaking it. Ruben Dumanovsky was here. I do not know if he beat me up or simply ordered it done. But he was supervising the enterprise."

"What did he want?"

"He wanted to know where the gold was."

"The treasure of Sheba?"

"The queen's hip chain. All of the queen's gold."

"What did you tell him."

"What could I tell him? I knew nothing. I pleaded with him to believe me. All I received was more brutality and further threats. He threatened to burn down Jebena. He threatened to burn down my flat, with my family inside."

"Do you have any idea why he didn't kill you?" Kobi could tell Kuur understood that his question was sincere.

"A good question. I thought he would. I think he believed I knew more than I did and that by watching me he would stand a greater chance of retrieving the treasure than he would by having me killed." Kuur tapped his fingers on his right armrest.

"Go on, Michael, what else?" Oscar encouraged him.

"He also said something to one of the men who was there."

"How many were there?" Cone interrupted ineptly.

"Three or four, I would guess, plus Dumanovsky," Kuur obliged. "He said something that made me believe he was upset with them for having killed the young man Kinga."

"What exactly did he say?" Kobi asked.

"He shouted at one point to one of them to stop beating me about the head. He yelled, 'Don't fuck this one up, too. You better not kill him.' The most shameful part of it for me was that, at that moment, I was thinking so solely for myself and for my own wellbeing that I was grateful. I was grateful for the intervention and to understand he did not desire for me to be murdered."

"You are quite sure it was Ruben Dumanovsky."

"As sure as I am that you are Mefake'ah Sambinsky."

Kobi rose and stretched. He walked once around the room, looking at the floor, at Oscar and at Cone, and finally again at Kuur.

"We are going to take your statement. You are going to sign it. Then I am going to arrest that criminal for attempted murder."

"Inspector—" Kuur objected, but the train had already initiated its departure from the station.

"I'd rather get him up for murder. But this will have to do for now. I can hold him, get him off the street, and isolate him while we continue the investigation. It will have to do."

Before Michael Kuur could protest any further, Kobi had picked up his phone to dial the prosecutor.

TWENTY-THREE

"I have one more call to make," Kobi said as they blinked in the sunshine.

A police car had pulled up, and Cone had briefed the young man inside to stay in position and watch for anyone looking like he might be from the Dumanovsky mob. Until he was arrested and booked, the danger level was extremely high.

Kobi walked four meters away to make his call. As he spoke, a huge smile crossed his face. When he was finished, he looked at Oscar. "Want to go do something fun?" He looked at Cone as if to say she wasn't invited. Oscar felt the most civilized thing for him to do would be to stay silent. But when Kobi turned to lead the way to his car, he followed.

Kobi drove up to Klausner Street and parked in front of the Rosenberg building. He stepped out, smoothed his hair, re-tucked his dress shirt into his slacks, and fished the sports jacket out of the back seat.

"Please tell me we are not putting on sports jackets and combing our hair to arrest Ruben Dumanovsky at Tel Aviv University." Oscar looked across the roof of the car at him. He thought he saw Kobi blush. "I had the impression that it was a matter of some urgency to place him under arrest. Has he taken an interest in higher education? Is he to be found here?"

"Cone is working through it with the State Attorney's office. Meanwhile, before I make a fool of myself on this investigation, I want to ask one expert about this so-called buried treasure."

Oscar smiled at him warmly enough to communicate he would choose to believe him but that he also understood there was some further reason Kobi had re-tucked his shirt three times.

Oscar could not help feeling self-conscious about his own appearance as they walked into the lobby and up the elevator to the first floor. It was the first time in his memory he was less formally dressed than Kobi, and it was the first time he could recall stepping onto a university campus without at least a freshly pressed everything. As they walked toward the end of the hallway, he understood they were about to visit an actual professor. He could not even bring himself to find it humorous that he felt so mortified. Even if the Israelis would hardly notice if he walked in wearing a t-shirt, he would notice. Nearly forty years of programming was mixed with an acute awareness that, no matter what anyone said or thought they thought, every single time he appeared anywhere in this country, he was carrying the entire continent of Africa on his shoulders and the aspirations of every single refugee. To dress well was to move his two worlds one centimeter closer together.

Tikkun Olam. He felt nauseous. *Okay,* he finally could grin, *that much is enough. You needn't vomit here in the hallway of the Jewish Studies Department. Not every single thing is the most important thing.*

Kobi stopped in front of Room 116. The name plate said "Professor Yael Rosenthal, Antiquities." Through the sidelight, Oscar could see a desk, a disarray of books and papers, chairs, lamps, and images of ancient objects and ruins postered on the walls. All the things he'd expect to see in an academic's office.

Kobi knocked, and a small, trim figure bounced into view and swung open the door.

"Kobi!" She threw open her arms and embraced him. "Kobi, Kobi, Kobi! How good to see you. I was so happy to hear your voice. What a treat!" They hugged for more than ten or twenty seconds. Kobi was gleaming like freshly polished copper.

"Who is your friend? Come in! Come on! Hello! My name is Yael." She spoke faster than a jet. "Come inside. Sit down! Never mind those! Move them. I'll move them. Oh, great. This is great! Great to see you!"

Oscar felt buoyed just being in the presence of their reunion. It was a maxim of his mother's that a good greeting could lift the entire village. Few people did greetings better than Israeli women.

He looked at Kobi and Yael as they arranged the office to sit. There was some enormous history here. Lives not lived, paths not taken. Even after so many years, he knew so little of his friend. Kobi looked instantly younger, his face sheepish and rakish, a youthful confidence and optimism glowing from him like an energy field.

And what a woman. A professor, smart, fast-talking, warm like a brioche. She was little, short, but she appeared ten times taller. Her life force could probably fill any room with anyone else in it. Her face and head were broad, and her features were defined in a mirror image of the busts you could find in the national museums. This woman was an Israelite. Her hair was up on top of her skull in a bun the size of a crown. Oscar furtively took a very fast glance at her hip set. *Oh, my,* he sighed to himself. *What can one do?* He looked at her fingers. She appeared unmarried. He looked over at Kobi. He was like a kid about to order ice cream.

"So? *Nu, nu, nu, nu, nu*? What then? What brings the Mefake'ah of the Israel Police to the Antiquities Department? Is someone looting?"

"Always," he answered.

"Do you know," and she turned to Oscar, " I have known this young man since elementary school. Don't you dare tell him how many years, Kobi. We went all the way through high school together."

Oscar smiled. He was truly delighted to learn something so personal about his friend. "What a marvelous reunion," he said warmly.

She bowed her head briefly in thanks. "Yes! We are true blue Haifanauts. They like to call us Haifaites, whatever the hell that means, sounds terrible, Haifaites. We know what to call ourselves. And we both made our way to the big city – long before it was the thing to do, you must know. And yet we see so little of each other nowadays. Why is that? It's a shame, of course."

"You're from Haifa?" Oscar asked, amazed and embarrassed that he had never bothered to ask. Kobi knew so much of his origins. Oscar wondered if he was too polite to have inquired or if he had just now learned that he was, somehow, a little self-centered. Shame washed over him.

"Yes, from Haifa. We are the Haifanauts. Yael and I and a few others in our gang. *L'chaim*." *To life*. He raised an imaginary glass.

"*L'chaim*," she agreed. "That reminds me. Coffee." She rose to get a machine going on her bookshelf.

"So, look, Yael, I need a reality check on something."

"I'm all ears."

"Have you ever heard of a secret treasure buried in the caves near Ein Bokek?"

"You mean apart from the Dead Sea Scrolls?" She raised her eyebrows to wait for him to feel dumb.

"Yes, apart from the Dead Sea Scrolls." He obliged her with a grin.

"Sure, sometimes. They've been digging around there for decades. It's a vast area. Every few years something pops up. Coins, scrolls, tablets, clothing, household wares. All of that."

"I mean something more specific. Have you ever come across a reference to a large hoard of gold and jewelry buried there at the time of Solomon?"

"At the time of Solomon?" She looked at the far wall searchingly.

"By the Queen of Sheba, maybe after her visit to Jerusalem? A treasure of her jewels that she buried there to keep safe for her eventual return. I know it sounds... "

"Well." Yael slumped back in her chair. "It's one of those things that comes up from time to time. Like a story or a myth. There are a good couple of dozen stories of great treasures kept secret since ancient times in a vault, in a cave, below a monastery, in the cistern of the Church of the Holy Sepulchre, below Al-Aqsa, in the desert, in the Western Wall foundations... This is one of those."

She stood and adjusted the coffee maker.

"On the Queen of Sheba story, there are pieces, fragments. A crusader knight who heard it from a Moor. A Mamluk lord who heard it sworn by a slave. The Sassanian captain who got it from a man begging for his life. One of Cyrus's governors who heard it from a widely traveled consort. But as a written record, no discovery, no clues in the actual sand, if you know what I mean."

Suddenly, she wheeled around and sat down in her desk chair facing them. "What's going on? Is someone trying to sell something claiming it is this secret treasure?" She looked suspicious and unhappy.

"No," Sambinsky said slowly. "Do you think your uncle would know something?"

She spat. "I still don't talk to that piece of shit. I haven't spoken to him in years. Even at my aunt's funeral. Every single day he breathes is a blight on my field and my family. That he owns the name J. Rosenthal is a *shanda*. Do you know how many fucking questions I had to answer when I was in my Ph.D. program, when I was up for appointments, when I was up for tenure? I still get them." She put her hand to her forehead. She looked at Oscar. "My uncle is Albi Rosenthal." She waited. "Are you an archaeologist?"

Oscar nearly felt flattered that she had not assumed he was police. He shook his head no. She tapped her fingers on her face.

"My uncle is a legendary shitbag in my field. He's an antiquities dealer. Which means half the stuff he sells is licensed under Israeli law, and the other ninety percent is black market patrimony. I'm sure he deals in fake stuff, too. He's the number one scrounger and sourcer of precious Jewish objects inside and outside Israel. The government seems to tolerate him for reasons G–d only knows. He's an unscrupulous rat. And he covers it all up in the most perfect Orthodox garb you can picture. It's revolting." She looked at Kobi. "No. No, I am not going to ask him."

"It's okay," he said. "This was plenty enough for now."

"I hope we can see each other sooner than three years." She smiled at him so warmly Oscar felt he was intruding simply by being present. He looked away.

"I do, too." They rose and embraced again. As Oscar was walking out the door, Kobi turned. "One more thing," he said. Oscar half hoped a declaration of love worthy of Frank Capra was about to be made. "If this story of a long-lost Queen of Sheba treasure were true, where would it have come from? I mean the gold. Where would she have gotten the gold?"

She put her hands on her hips and looked up at him, standing ten centimeters closer than she probably had to. Perhaps she had been wishing for Capra, too.

"Probably Abyssinia or the Nile area. Nowadays Ethiopia, Egypt, Sudan. Why? You found something?"

"No, Yael, not yet. I'm still looking." He hugged her again, they said they'd see each other soon, and he led Oscar down the hallway.

It must have been a pleasure to see such a good old friend, Oscar wanted to say as they reached the street. But even that felt too saucy to him. Kobi could have – might well have – snorted, to show he knew exactly what Oscar was actually asking. But Oscar didn't feel he could say nothing. Too much had just happened. His poker face wasn't that good. And besides, it must be more gracious to acknowledge something about what he'd learned.

"I didn't realize you were from Haifa," he blurted as they settled back into the car. He immediately felt how feeble it was.

Kobi snorted.

TWENTY-FOUR

I t was an inconvenient time for this kind of operation. People would be leaving work and beginning to throng the cafés, shops and pubs that lined every inch of Allenby. An appearance of a couple of heavily armed uniforms would not disturb anyone in Israel. That was normal. No one would bat an eyelash. But bring eight men all at once in the middle of Tel Aviv, long guns up and flak jackets on, and the citizens might run and scream for fear of an anti-terrorist action.

They had planned it accordingly. Sambinsky had chosen *Rav Samal Mitkadem* First Sergeant Yehoshua Gridstein to lead. Gridstein was former Shayetet 13, an Israeli Navy SEAL, and an officer – as he would remind Kobi, he was "the one with the plan, not the one with the knife." He was the savviest operator in Salameh 18 when it came to fast, low profile raids. By the time 5 p.m. had rolled around, Cone had secured the warrant, Gridstein had prepped his team, and Sambinsky had received approval for the plan from the Deputy.

Before six o'clock, the van was sitting twenty meters from the door to the Pasternak Design Build Develop office. An undercover had been across the street drinking coffee for four hours already and had confirmed that someone answering Dumanovsky's description was to be seen at the window and that for sure no one looking like him had left the office since his surveillance had begun. He confirmed that several other people had left the building since shortly after five. A second undercover had circled the block until finding an appropriate parking spot and occupied the space until the van arrived.

Sambinsky hoped no one would notice it was a baker's van. It was perfect for morning operations, but it didn't fit in the afternoon commute. Anyone expert who was paying attention would wonder, and Dumanovsky was expert enough and attentive enough. But the two other tactical vans they kept at Salameh 18, the wireless utility truck and the crappy blue nondescript warehouse one, were out of the shed for whatever reasons, and Kobi hadn't wanted to lose three hours requisitioning another from a different location.

"Stop it." Gridstein looked Cone in the eyes briefly, enough to get her attention but not embarrass her. "The sound carries." He glanced at her foot, and back at her face. She ceased bouncing her sole on the van floor. She was breathing hard and perspiring. She didn't like small, crowded spaces. There were nine bodies in the cargo bay of the vehicle. The pressure and seriousness of the operation had been mounting all day. This wasn't just an arrest. They were planning for the possibility of sophisticated armed resistance. She hadn't worn a helmet since leaving the academy.

Gridstein gave his team the instructions once again. The plan was to open the van doors, exit quietly, move to the exterior wall of the buildings on the street so as to avoid casual detection from the windows above, and slide quickly and silently along the buildings until reaching the door. The executive officer, Yariv Feldman, would open the glass door to the staircase. Gridstein himself would lead the way to the second level. The office was called Pasternak Design Build Develop. Mefake'ah Sambinsky would execute the door knock. Gridstein would be next to him. Both men would stand at the edges of the door in case there was spontaneous fire coming from inside. Sambinsky believed the door was steel, but no point in taking chances. Immediately after the door knock, Sambinsky would withdraw to make room for Avi Fleyder. Right behind Avi would be Zeev Rabinowsky with the Blackhawk battering ram in case no one was opening the door voluntarily. "As soon as the door opens," Gridstein ordered, "I will go in first, Avi next. Zeev will stand aside with the battering ram. Sambinsky comes in third. Everyone is to be immobilized and on the ground immediately. Oren and Uri will search the rooms. We count three rooms and a toilet. Check closets and under desks. All we want is Ruben Dumanovsky, but we will arrest anyone else who wants to be arrested. Absolutely no shooting without imminent threat. Officer Cone, will you be comfortable making space for Officer Feldman to enter last, and then you can please come in right after him? If a civilian appears in the stairwell, I don't want a panic." She nodded silently and was grateful. He had read the situation perfectly. "Mr. Orleans, I understand you are going to stay here?"

"Yes, thank you," Oscar said, feeling like an idiot in the helmet they had insisted he put on. It fit poorly, covering far more of his head than was intended. He could hear his heart pounding in his ears. Kobi's insistence that "this will be great" had given him no comfort. He would be far happier sweltering in the van by himself listening for gunfire he hoped wouldn't come.

Gridstein spoke into his sleeve mic to the undercover at the café. "All clear," he reported to the team. "Okay, let's go."

They were lined up against the building wall and running toward the door in single file before anyone on the street could take adequate notice. The passersby were starting to look up from their phones by the time they reached the glass door. One woman yanked her kid out of their way. Kobi was impressed by her presence of mind.

Feldman held the door as planned, and they were up the stairs in less than half a minute. Kobi felt fatter than ever. Gridstein's breathing had barely changed. The boots on the stairs ricocheted off the walls. The entire building must have heard. Kobi looked at Yehoshua, who nodded. No time to lose. Knock right now.

"POLICE! Open up! We have a warrant. POLICE!"

Kobi stepped back and the massive Avi took his place in a lunge position. The still more massive Zeev Rabinowsky stepped right behind him, holding the Blackhawk ram in the backswing in case Gridstein gave him the order.

The door opened. Before the crack had reached six centimeters and before a face was clearly visible, Gridstein crushed it open with his shoulder and flew inside. Avi was right behind him.

"Get down! Get down! On the floor! Hands where we can see them."

Kobi was third inside. Crumpled on the hard wood was the young blonde woman he had seen at the conference table. Her hand covered her face, catching some amount of blood that had appeared when the door struck her. She had been the unlucky one to answer the knock. She was mewling, cursing.

The team streamed in behind Kobi. "Hands in the air!" someone shouted at the squat old woman sitting behind the reception. She didn't move, but Kobi could see her lips wanted to curl. She was seething.

Gridstein kicked open the private office door and pointed his carbine inside. Ruben Dumanovsky was already standing in the middle of the room, his hands high and visible. He wasn't planning on getting killed.

"Clear!" The voices of the team carried. "Clear!" they shouted as they verified the suite was otherwise empty.

"All clear," Feldman confirmed to Gridstein.

"Ruben Dumanovsky, you are under arrest for the attempted murder of Michael Alou Kuur Kuur," Sambinsky said as he placed Dumanovsky's hands into cuffs. "You have no rights whatsoever, you Armenian fuck, and it would be my great pleasure to kill you if you attempt to escape," he whispered in his ear. Dumanovsky attempted a grin, but Kobi could see it wasn't the real thing.

"Don't even think about it," Kobi heard Cone say as they led Dumanovsky into the waiting area. Cone was pointing her service weapon at the squat receptionist, who was reaching, furtively, behind her desk for something, perhaps a drawer.

"No, mama, don't," Dumanovsky said quickly.

"Mama!" Kobi laughed. "Mama Dumanovsky! Hahahahaha!"

Cone shoved the woman back and opened two drawers before she found an automatic pistol. She grabbed it and checked its safety and placed it in her belt.

"Well, well, well, Ruben, looks like you and mama are both going to wear government pajamas," Sambinsky said as loud as he could. "Does your girlfriend want to do something, too? Perhaps she wants to join you?"

The young woman looked up at him and spat blood on the floor.

TWENTY-FIVE

"Abune, perhaps it would be more convenient for us to speak in one of the cells?" Oscar spoke quietly, his hand near his hat to afford further protection from the sun.

"I am hardly Abune, Oscar, as you know." The old man smiled back at him, speaking slowly and no more loudly than another man's whisper.

"Father, perhaps—"

"You may call me Paulos," he interrupted, waving his hand slowly. "Or depending on the nature of your business, you may call me by my given name, which is Tewodros." He grinned impishly. It was impossible not to like this old monk.

"Paulos, please, perhaps it would be more private to speak in one of the cells."

"Oscar, the last thing anyone cares about in this country is what two skinny Africans are discussing."

Oscar reset his feet. He had come to Deir es Sultan on top of the Church of the Holy Sepulchre to find Father Paulos the Ethiopian Monk. He was behaving exactly as Oscar had remembered.

"Paulos, I am here to make an inquiry in my function as liaison to the Israel Police. I will make it here if you insist, but please understand if I speak quietly." Here was the narrow passage outside the miniscule Ethiopian chapel. For centuries, the Coptic and Ethiopian officiates had been battling over the tiny rooms built on top of the massive Armenian chapel of St. Helena. Once every few decades, one group forcibly seized it from the other. Since the 1970s, the Ethiopians possessed the monastery, but the Copts always placed a monk in a chair a few meters away just in case. A handful of tourists milled about to take in the beauty and the eccentricities. Oscar had to agree no one was likely to listen. And in any case his final oblique attempt to persuade the old monk had failed. Paulos just offered him an idiotic smile. It was a terrifically effective form of condescension.

"Have you ever seen this man?" Oscar held up his phone. Paulos gazed at it, then lifted his hand to hold it up and move it under the eaves of the monastery to get the benefit of shadow. Since Dumanovsky's arrest, Mefake'ah Sambinsky had been trying to connect him to Father Kinga Longokwo explicitly, so he could build affirmative cases for murder. He had asked Oscar to go back in time to Longokwo's visit to Israel. No doubt the former priest had visited the holy sites in Jerusalem. And anyone looking for Africans who had visited the Church of the Holy Sepulchre would do well to go see the Ethiopian monks. And that was Oscar's department.

The monk's face drew into a look of recognition. The old man was trying to place a ghost he was recalling from somewhere, some time.

"Perhaps twelve years ago? He was called Father Kinga Longokwo. He would have been visiting from Sudan with a delegation of East African clergymen."

"Oh yes! I do remember." Paulos smiled widely, perhaps at the pleasure of recall, which, at his age, may have been pleasure enough. Oscar waited in case there was more. "He took the Latin rites. He was a Catholic. Not Orthodox. No, no, he was a Catholic."

"Yes, I believe that is correct. At one time he was a Catholic priest," Oscar said, feeling immediately that he had said too much.

"Oh, really? He was, but no longer?" Paulos had almost nothing to do all day save pray and contemplate and remain in place lest any marauding Copts seek a territorial incursion. It was dangerous to permit too wide a sidebar. One could get lost in it for hours.

"What can you recall of meeting him?" Oscar asked.

"He came with other Africans. You are right. Africans coming to visit Jerusalem. Mostly Sudanese. Mostly Christians of the Anglican or Roman Catholic churches, some Copts, some Orthodox. They came to tour the church, to pray. Of course we met with them. They always trot out the Africans to meet Africans." Paulos and Oscar allowed themselves to share a smile. "I spoke with him. We talked about our work. He was very interesting and informed about the tragedy then unfolding for his people. But I was also struck by his optimism." He tapped his right hand on his left arm as he continued to remember details of their encounter. "They were not alone, in fact. They had the usual tour guides. But their group of fifteen or so East Africans was joined by a handful of Israelis, too."

That was why Oscar had come. He tried hard not to lean forward visibly. "Who were they?" he asked.

"They were Israelis who had an interest in East Africa. They were people who knew people or who knew enough of East Africa to make the visitors feel welcome and to make business and spiritual connections that might outlast the trip. You know how these things go, Oscar. The Israelis are so outmatched in diplomacy. They must use every occasion they have to forge bonds with visitors from other countries."

"Was this one of the Israelis? Do you recognize him?" He held up his phone again. Paulos squinted. "His name is Ruben Dumanovsky. Does that help?"

"He looks so young here," Paulos said.

"You have seen him?" Oscar felt a wave of urgency.

"I do not know his name. But I have seen him before. He might have been with that group. I do not know."

"Paulos, I am here because the Israel Police have asked me to speak with Africans who may have met these two men together when Father Longokwo visited Israel twelve years ago. The police believe he did a clergy tour, and it is believed he met this Dumanovsky on that trip. We suspect they may have been here at the same time. It is very important to try to remember if you saw them together."

"Well, I do recognize him. I know his face."

Oscar looked intently at him. "What do you mean?"

"I have seen him more than once."

"When?"

"My son, he is here often. Probably several times per year." Paulos was old enough that Oscar found himself wondering about his memory.

"You mean at Deir es Sultan?" Oscar was grasping for a place to put the news.

"No, moron," the monk said to him slowly. "In the church." He pointed to the roof below their feet.

"In the Armenian chapel?" Oscar asked, his eyes roving for a spot to fix them while he puzzled it out. At least Kobi would be pleased to learn Dumanovsky had an interest in Armenia after all.

"No, Oscar. Latin rites. This man is a Catholic."

Oscar was suddenly aware of his own silence and of the

magnificent silence of the rooftop. A bird flew overhead. Otherwise there was not a sound to be heard except for gentle echoes from the street level. This odd corner of Jerusalem was indeed glorious. It was undoubtedly a precious perch from which to consider the sacred and even the profane.

"How fares your soul, Oscar?" Paulos asked after what Oscar realized must have been a long minute.

The question hit him in the chest like a truck. In this setting, in this moment, after this week of speed and terror, coming from this man of G–d, it was too much to take. He felt his chest heave. He forced air down his throat to steady himself.

"Have you found G–d among the Jews?" Paulos asked. Silence followed again. In the corner of his eye, Oscar could see the Coptic monk adjust his cassock over his legs.

"I believe I have found my home," he replied at last.

"Then you are well found, Brother Oscar. I am proud of you. *Baruch HaShem.*" *Blessed is the Name.*

"Thank you, Father." He smiled slowly and felt a surge of warmth in his body for the first time in days. It did seem to him true that G–d lived more accessibly in some cities, some buildings, some people, some encounters. He continued in a whisper. "Would you tell me, please, how you came to believe this man is a Catholic?"

"What do you want? He prays among the Catholics. He spends time with the priests. He takes the sacraments. I believe he is especially close to a Ukrainian Catholic priest who has some privileges here via the Roman accommodation. They can be so accommodating with people of the book. Especially if they are white."

"Kobi," Oscar said into his phone as he reached the stone paving of the St. Helena Street. "I believe Hanukah comes early for you this year."

TWENTY-SIX

"Guess what, you lowlife sack of shit." Kobi Sambinsky was in perhaps his favorite pose. He pressed his hands on the table across from Dumanovsky in the jail interview room. Dumanovsky was already wearing the drab olive uniform of the prison population. His estimable lawyer sat next to him. Behind Sambinsky, Cone stood against the wall in her battle stance, and Oscar tried to look relaxed while feeling far more vulnerable than he knew himself to be.

Kobi loved these moments. He loved the sensation of insulting a perp while feeling that his own blood pressure was nice and easy. He felt like this only when a hard case was about to come to an end, when he had all the leverage he needed to get it sealed and delivered for good.

"You're going away, shitsucker. You're going away forever." Dumanovsky looked confused. His lawyer was endeavoring to look unimpressed. "You and your street-whore-slut-mother, too. You're both going away forever. Son and slut. Together till the end."

"What the fuck you talking about?" Dumanovsky spat

through his teeth. Gangsters were all the same. Never call their mothers sluts. It was worse than chopping off their fingers.

"Oh, sorry? Don't remember?" Kobi languorously opened a file and distributed photocopies. "You and your slut-mother both filled these out." The lawyer looked at the paper and up at Dumanovsky. Oscar thought he caught a look of disgust on the lawyer's face. "You and whoremom lied on your immigration applications." Dumanovsky's face had changed. "You swore – you see there? – you swore you were both Jews. You were admitted as citizens under the Right of Return. But guess what? You are both Catholic! Yep! Mother and son both baptized Ukrainian Catholics. As was your dear departed prison-bottom dad. All confirmed. Your grandparents, too. And how about that? You're not Russian. You're not even Armenian. You're straight multi-generational Ukrainian. You pretended to be Russian Jews and let just enough smoke make a trail for Armenia in case we ever wanted to look. Just to lead us away from Ukraine. It was very smart. But you're a straight fucking Ukrainian criminal sack of shit from a criminal sack of shit family. All sacks of shit for generation upon generation. And not a drop of Jew in you. Yet look at all of this great stuff on your applications. Your Hebrew names, your Jewish history, your family's lineage. All bullshit. You came here as Jews, and we let you in so you could be safe to live as Jews. But you're as Jewish as Pontius Pilate sucking a hog's cock."

Dumanovsky looked stunned. His lawyer understood that somehow, whatever happened from here, his client was finished.

"You know, all these years, the police were trying to connect to Armenia. We thought you weren't Jewish, but you had us barking up the wrong tree. It turns out you're a Ukrainian Catholic pretending to be an Armenian pretending to be a Jew. Go figure."

"It's not illegal in this country to worship according to your conscience." Dumanovsky's lawyer spoke up.

"Shut up, pigface," Kobi answered without looking at him. "You'll have a chance to try to explain to a judge. As far as I see it, this one is simple. There are a few people in Ukraine who want to talk to Ruben. Whoreson and whoremother leave for Ukraine on a flight under custody and never come back. All of their assets in Israel are immediately forfeit. Or he faces prosecution for attempted murder and then gets deported after he rots in jail. Either way, he's going back to Ukraine. We don't house diarrhea-faced sacks of mucus from Ukraine in our country. Or their street-trick mothers. Not unless they are Jews."

He turned to leave.

"I am a Catholic," Dumanovsky said. "You of all people should understand. Catholics in Ukraine are persecuted, purged. Can't go to school. Can't get jobs. Jews of all the countries should understand how hard it is to be harangued and massacred." Kobi looked at him. It was the first authentic-seeming feeling he had seen on Dumanovsky's face. "I have helped Catholics. In Sudan I have helped Catholics. Here I have helped Catholics. In Ukraine, too. All over Africa the Muslims are killing Christians. Catholics especially suffer in South Sudan. Yes. I lied on my immigration. But ever since I have worked to save Catholics, to make safe places for Catholics to pray and live. You cannot imagine how terrible it was in Ukraine, Mefake'ah. When I got opportunity, I swore to make life better for Catholics in places they suffer. Every day I think about it."

Oscar noticed Kobi's shoulders soften. He also felt affected. Dumanovsky's face was sincere. In whatever manner this man could muster, he did feel he was on a mission, one worthy of consideration, especially by a nation existentially familiar with persecution.

"*Fihnya.*" *Bullshit.* Angelika spoke in Ukrainian. "I am from

Ukraine. I am Jewish. Catholics beat us up when we were kids. Catholics killed our families just like Orthodox. You are just regular piece of shit criminal. Enjoy the rest of your short shitty life back home. You will be in prison within a month or dead within a week. I will light a candle for the people you murdered."

TWENTY-SEVEN

O scar strolled into Jebena. He had felt increasingly relaxed over the past two days. The deportation proceeding was underway. Dumanovsky was not contesting it. He probably thought it was better to take his chances on the streets of Kiev and with a corruptible local prosecutor than to sit in an Israeli jail cell.

Kuur's bandages were removed. Bruising and ugly lacerations remained. He sat in his throne and waved Oscar inside.

"Oscar, Oscar!" he said. "Guhwah, please, for my friend!"

The response of the room was more muted than the pastor's. Oscar could sense the trepidation that now followed his arrival. There had been a lot of police and a lot of yelling since the investigation had started. The refugees who found respite here needed little of either.

The old lady shuffled to his cushion and handed him a steaming cup. Oscar felt she gave it to him a little too forcefully. A drop spilled on his finger. It burned hotly for a brief second.

He looked up at her. She had been waiting for him to do so. Her eyes met his.

"No justice for refugees," she said to him. The mix of menace and helpless resentment was all over her face.

So that was it. Apart from Kuur, they did not want him here today. For them, Oscar was the police. The police had traded a deportation for a murder case and possibly two. Oscar understood the logic, but he also understood the miss. Dumanovsky would be gone soon. His gang would be gutted, some murdered by his own hand and the rest leaderless and imminently bereft of money. Pastor Kuur and his family were safe. South Sudanese would not have to fear him. But no one would answer for the murder of the Shabbat Kinga. That was true. It was hard to imagine the Israeli police would have done the same for an Israeli.

But it was also hard to imagine a better outcome for the innocent people still alive. *And wasn't that the story of this country?* he thought to himself.

"Is there ever any?" he asked the lady out loud. She bowed and allowed a small smile and shuffled back to the pot.

"Pastor Michael, I should go." He rose, still holding his cup.

"I shall come with you." Kuur breathed in through his nose and pushed himself to his feet. He picked up a cane leaning against the chair and walked uneasily toward the door. He put his other arm through Oscar's to steady himself.

"Thank you," he said as they stood on the desolate street, the quiet punctuated by a small motorbike engine somewhere down the block.

Oscar inhaled. He decided he must ask. "Michael, why did it take you so long to tell us about Dumanovsky?"

"He was threatening—"

"I mean before that. Why did you never tell anyone what he was doing to you? What he was doing to the Sudanese. What you thought he did to the young man Kinga from eight years ago."

"You don't know?" Kuur asked. His eyes implored him not to make him say it.

"I believe... Michael, please tell me, in confidence. I would hate myself if my conjecture were wrong."

Kuur looked down the street. "I loved him. That young man was the first love of my life. He remains the only one I have ever known."

Oscar nodded, though Kuur wasn't looking at him.

"You know how it is with us. I have hidden my sin my entire life. I was never able to love or touch the way I wanted. At home, it was impossible. Here, the Israelis accept it. But even here I could not. The immigration bureau would have surmised I had HIV. They would have humiliated me. My parishioners – such as I have them –" he smiled broadly at himself – "would have rejected me. Then eight years ago out of the blue this young man arrived. He was... breathtaking. So beautiful, so energetic, so full of passion. A young brave knight on a quest for family and for his people. I was on fire for him. Then one night late we were here, in Jebena, and we were alone. My wildest dreams were answered. He kissed me. I can still feel it. My life changed. The next weeks were the best of my life." He looked at Oscar. "But then Dumanovsky came. That monster. Kinga could not help provoking him. Dumanovsky showed up here, threw around his weight. It was ugly. But it was far uglier when he showed me what he had gathered. His men had started following Kinga everywhere he went. Everywhere he slept. How he held hands. How he embraced. The photographs are indelible in my mind. I was not the only one. Of course I was jealous. He had young lovers. White lovers. He would have. He was so attractive. But the photographs of us were terrifying. Dumanovsky knew from then on I would be... compliant. That I would become... his slave."

"You are no one's slave," Oscar said crisply. "You are free now."

"Am I?" Kuur asked. At the corner of the block, Lily and Nellie came into view. Kuur sighed deeply. Oscar could only guess what it meant.

TWENTY-EIGHT

"I'll take an Americano, too," Kobi said to the waitress. She sauntered toward the inside coffee bar. He caught Oscar looking. "Nice ass," he said.

"Great hips," Oscar replied.

The sun was starting to set. Orange giving way to pink and red blazed across the simmering sea. Hints of October chill floated amidst the top notes of the air.

"It's still out there," Kobi said.

"It must be."

"Are you going to look for it?"

"Are you?"

"Come on," Kobi grinned. "Imagine that conversation with the chief."

Oscar smiled back and let the last moments of sunshine kiss his face.

"I have a son," Kobi said.

Oscar sat up. He was reminded of how little Kobi had told him about himself and of how little he had asked. He was aware that Kobi had a son, but he was sure more was about to be forthcoming.

"He's in the Sayeret. Every night I stay awake as late as I can till he lets me know he is back from a patrol."

"That must be a great burden," Oscar said slowly. He felt their friendship had just locked one more set of arms.

The waitress brought Kobi's Americano. He sipped it, and, as if in a commercial, raised the glass and smiled approvingly. Oscar chuckled.

"Kobi, I apologize that I have not done a better job of inquiring about your life. Perhaps I could have been a better friend."

"Not at all. I'm the asshole."

"Why would you say that?"

"All these years, after all the help you've given me, us, the police – have I ever done what I really could to help you with your asylum petition?"

Oscar didn't know what to say.

"Of course I haven't. I barely did anything. I just figured... I don't know what I figured. That justice would take its course. But year followed year after year. And then... this piece of shit Dumanovsky. I can do so much more for you. I will do it. I kept thinking these past days. How does that guy get to be an Israeli and you don't?"

"Through dishonesty, Kobi," Oscar said.

"*Nachon.*"

Michael Fertik lives in California.